I0577626

# FRIDAY I'M IN LOVE

## WILD IRISH, BOOK 5

## MARI CARR

Copyright © 2016 by Mari Carr

All rights reserved.

No part of this book may be reproduced in any form or by any electronic or mechanical means, including information storage and retrieval systems, without written permission from the author, except for the use of brief quotations in a book review.

*This story is dedicated to my cousins. I never had a sister, but I was blessed with lots and lots of girl cousins who were definitely the next best thing! I love you gals!*

## PRAISE FOR FRIDAY I'M IN LOVE

"There were so many **laugh out loud moments** in this books. I really loved it, and this whole family." ★★★★★ *Staci, Goodreads*

"**Best** of the Series!" ★★★★★ *Sassafrass, Goodreads*

"I even **teared** up at the end, it was that sweet!" ★★★★★ *MountainKat, Goodreads*

"This story is **funny**, **hot** and **filled with hope**!" ★★★★★ *Sylvie Rochon, Goodreads*

"**I can't say enough** about this series!" ★★★★★ *Jenna, Goodreads*

"***sigh***...it's so gorgeous!" ★★★★ *Christi Snow, Goodreads*

"This is an entertaining, exciting, sweet and hot story and, yes, you will cry for these two, but you will have **that warm and fuzzy feeling at the end** - awesome story!" ★★★★ *Dar, Goodreads*

"I think this was my **favorite** book in the series thus far." ★★★★ *Kimberly, Goodreads*

# PLAYLIST

Fans of Spotify! Now you can access the Wild Irish "titles" playlist.

Come Monday – Jimmy Buffett
Ruby Tuesday – The Rolling Stones.
Waiting for Wednesday – Lisa Loeb and Nine Stories.
Sweet Thursday – Matt Costa
Friday I'm in Love – The Cure
Saturday Night Special – Lynard Skynard
Any Given Sunday – Sandpeople

# MONDAY'S CHILD

Monday's child is fair of face,
Tuesday's child is full of grace,
Wednesday's child is full of woe,
Thursday's child has far to go,
Friday's child is loving and giving,
Saturday's child works hard for a living,
But the child who is born on the Sabbath day,
Is bonny and blithe and good and gay.

*~Traditional nursery rhyme*

# CHAPTER ONE

"You're the life of the party." Sky Mitchell claimed the seat beside her and she rolled her eyes at his droll comment.

"It's a freaking kid's birthday party."

Sky laughed. "That's not stopping anybody else."

Natalie Miller glanced around Pat's Irish Pub and admitted he was right. The Collins family—apparently true to their Irish heritage—were partying it up in style. Several of the men were hanging out around the bar, consuming pints of Guinness, while the ladies were chattering and laughing loudly over their glasses of wine. She sighed. "Guess I'm just not in the mood."

"Yeah, I noticed. You haven't been in the mood to have fun for quite a while. What gives?"

"Nothing gives. I think I'm just starting to feel my age."

Sky laughed again. "You're only thirty-four. Hell,

I'm the same age as you and I've never felt better in my life."

"I'm sure that has nothing to do with the fact you're banging Miss Sunshine and Peace Signs Collins every night."

"You're gonna have to stop giving Teagan shit about being a hippie."

Natalie raised an eyebrow. "Have you seen the way she dresses?"

Sky shrugged. "I love her wardrobe. It's hot."

"Oh Jesus, you're pathetic. Besides, getting older is different for men." She wasn't sure that was true, but it sounded plausible enough. "It's a well-known fact men never grow up."

"So you've been walking around with a stick up your ass for the last three months because you suddenly think you're old?"

She didn't know how to tell Sky he'd basically summed it up perfectly. Leave it to her to have a midlife crisis at thirty-four. Who fell apart on their thirty-fourth birthday?

"Not old, necessarily. Just older." She'd been in a funk since she'd blown out the single candle her business partner, Christine, had stuck in a Hostess Twinkie to celebrate yet another year in an otherwise unexceptional life. She'd spent the remainder of her birthday taking pictures at an elderly couple's silver anniversary party. She'd listened as their children, grandchildren, friends and colleagues praised the couple's long and glorious union.

She'd gotten home well after midnight, crawled into bed and cried her eyes out.

"Oh, well, that clears up everything." Sky's tone was sardonic and she chuckled. One of the reasons they got along so well was because they both had only two tones, sarcastic and sarcastic. Although now that Sky was doing the horizontal mamba with Teagan Collins, he'd added romantic to his repertoire. An idea that bugged the hell out of Natalie.

"You sure you wanna stay here this week? I know you've attended Collins celebrations before, but staying with them for an entire week could be tough for you."

She filled in the blanks on the things her friend was too polite to say out loud. He didn't think she'd enjoy staying with the Collins family because that would involve her being in close contact with other people for more than a few hours. Sky knew she preferred her solitary existence because her interpersonal skills were more than slightly lacking.

She'd taken a month-long working vacation away from her photography business to hit the road with Sky. He'd invited her to travel around with him to take some behind-the-scenes pictures of him and Teagan as they toured. They'd told everyone it was for a photo-biography she was compiling, but the truth was, Sky wanted to surprise Teagan with a special video as a wedding gift. Natalie had been snapping photos of the couple for three weeks straight, trying to capture some really perfect moments in their lives together. He planned to play the video at their wedding reception.

The word *romantic* floated through her mind again and she did an internal eye roll.

She'd jumped at Sky's offer to escape her ho-hum life, thinking travel would lure her out of her doldrums. It had certainly worked in the past. It wasn't unusual for her to leave the business in Christine's capable hands while she got away for a bit to try to get her shit together, try to overcome her dark moods. Unfortunately, this time the escape hadn't worked. She wasn't any happier now than before she'd hit the road. If anything, she was in a deeper funk.

"I'll be fine with the Collins family. Besides, Teagan's going to be working on wedding preparations and we agreed it would be cool to get some pictures of her with her family as they got ready for the big day."

"Yeah, well. I'm worried about you, Nat. This feels like," he paused, "last time."

She grinned and tried to mask the agony his words provoked. She was worried about herself too. She felt so sad, so heavy, so adrift…but these weren't feelings she wanted to admit. She'd succumbed to the darkness only once before and she was *not* going back there.

"I'm fine, Sky. Promise. It's not the same as last time. This will pass."

"Sky, come on. Let's give Caitlyn her gift," Teagan called out to her fiancé.

Natalie waved him off as he rose. "Wouldn't do to keep Princess Catie waiting," she teased. It was safe to say no child had ever been more doted on or adored than Caitlyn Wallace, Teagan's niece. A glance at the food table confirmed this as Natalie shook her head once again at the colorful cupcake castle dominating the table.

"You know, I never told you my birthday wish for you," Sky said. They'd started the silly tradition back in high school. On their birthdays, each made a wish for the other.

"Still trying to top my wish?" On Sky's eighteenth birthday, she'd wished for him to become the most famous musician in the world. She claimed the wish had worked. God knew he was certainly on his way toward reaching that level of stardom.

"I wished for you to fall in love and live happily ever after."

"You didn't," she hissed. She'd always forbidden that wish in the past, claiming she didn't need or want a man to interfere with her life or career.

"I did," Sky replied, kissing her on the cheek. "Happy belated birthday, Nat."

He walked away and she shook her head, feeling the slightest kernel of panic building in her chest. It was a silly tradition. It's not as if their wishes always came true or anything. She was a fool for sitting here with a racing heart and sweaty palms just because of Sky's stupid wish. Jesus, she really was losing her mind.

"Okay, I give. What the hell is up with you?"

Natalie looked up and found Ewan Collins standing beside her table. "Was there a two-for-one deal on that line somewhere and I missed it? I'm gonna tell you what I just told Sky. Nothing's wrong with me. Now get lost."

He smiled and ignored her request, claiming the

seat Sky had vacated. She steadfastly ignored the heat suddenly permeating her skin at his proximity. It was always the same any time he was within five feet of her. Her body went into serious overdrive. She resisted the urge to fan herself and blamed it on a hot flash. Early onset menopause. Sure. That could be it.

"You've been moping around all day. It's a party, and you've done nothing but sit and nurse the same glass of wine. So I'll repeat my question. What the hell is up with you?"

Natalie scowled. Ewan had been a thorn in her side since the night they'd met—the night of Sky's final concert with his previous group, The Universe. Though they'd spent less than a month's worth of days together in the past three years, she typically spent weeks thinking about him and their conversations after each visit. His pursuit of her had been relentless, so she had to give him points for persistence.

"You know," she said, deciding evasion was her best bet. "I just don't get you."

He grinned and wiggled his eyebrows. "That's because I'm an enigma. Even my own family doesn't know what to make of me."

She ignored his jest. "I'm fairly certain I've made my feelings for you clear. Have I not?" She had him age-wise by nearly a decade and to say she was typically a total bitch whenever they were together was probably putting it lightly.

Ewan nodded. "If you mean telling me *get lost, go fuck myself* and *you are the most annoying man I've ever met,* then yes, I think all of that was pretty straightforward."

"And yet here you sit." She gestured at him, letting her irritation show.

"That's because I know you don't mean any of that."

She raised one eyebrow. "I don't?"

He shook his head. "Your words say go away, but your eyes say come closer." He punctuated that inane comment by leaning toward her. She tried to force her body to move away or, at the very least, shove his ass out of the booth, but found herself trying to covertly sneak a sniff of his scent. She wasn't sure what it was about his smell that attracted her so. She could detect the slight odor of the beer he'd been drinking on his breath. And damn, if she didn't feel her mouth watering for a taste.

"This is insane," she muttered to herself, surprised when his grin grew.

"Nope. It's chemistry."

"I'm too old for you." It was her standard fallback line. The one she'd used time after time to push him away.

He rested his forehead against hers intimately and again she wondered why she never tore into him for his inappropriate familiarity. They didn't know each other well enough for him to crowd her personal space like this, and yet, she never resisted when he grabbed her hand to hold, never shrugged him off when he wrapped a friendly arm around her shoulder.

"I'm twenty-six to your thirty-four. Eight years, Nat. That's all. That excuse is lame. Why don't you try to find a new one?"

"How about I'm not interested?"

He smiled. "Well, now you're just lying."

She scowled and moved her face away from his, frustration growing in her chest. "It is taking every ounce of strength in my body not to throw you through a wall right now."

He laughed and put his arm against the back of the booth, caging her in. "Oh babydoll. I'd love to see that."

She knew her threat was empty. While she was nearly five foot nine, the top of her head barely cleared his shoulders when they were standing. Unlike his brothers—who were built like goliath football players, Ewan was lankier, his build reminding her more of a basketball player. A basketball player with rock-hard abs and muscular arms that could hold a woman against a wall and—

She closed her eyes and forced the naughty fantasy away. Damn man was starring in more of her wet dreams lately than Gerard Butler. She cleared her throat and gave him a narrow-eyed scowl. "Babydoll is a sexist term and I find it highly offensive."

"No you don't."

She clenched her fists and fought the urge to strike him. "Stop telling me what I think!"

"You finished dodging the subject at hand?"

She threw in the towel. She didn't have the energy for this. "I'm just tired." Her answer was weak, but it wasn't entirely untrue. She was averaging five hours of restless sleep a night, if she was lucky.

"Why are you tired?"

She closed her eyes and prayed for patience. This was how conversations with Ewan went. He asked a question, she answered, and then he asked more.

"I was reading a really sexy book last night and spent half the night masturbating with my vibrator. All those amazing orgasms can really take it out of you, you know?" She hoped her smartass comment would embarrass him, shut him up.

She should have known better.

"Shit, Nat. I wish you would have waited. I'm going to be downstairs from you tonight. I can fuck you a helluva lot better than a lousy piece of plastic."

She'd been given Tristan's old room on the third floor to sleep in while she was staying with the family, but sleep didn't seem to be something she was going to be doing much of, especially not after the sexy seed Ewan had just planted.

"In your dreams, kiddo. I don't play with children," she said, although she wasn't all that concerned that he was younger.

For one thing, he didn't act young, but she supposed that was because he'd been responsible—along with his sister, Keira—for running the restaurant side of his family's business since graduating from college. Teagan raved about his management abilities and smooth administration. The fun, sexually explicit banter he engaged in with Natalie seemed to be the exception, rather than the norm, and she got the feeling the rest of his family saw him as serious, responsible, staid.

"Thought you weren't gonna play the age card again?"

"Old habits die hard."

"You're quiet today, distant. Why do I get the feeling it's more than fatigue?"

"I would think you'd be glad I'm quiet. I mean, it's not as if there's ever been any love lost between us. You and I are like—"

He looked so genuinely shocked she stopped midsentence, the words *oil and water* dying on her tongue.

"No love lost? I'm *crazy* about you, Nat. You must know that?"

She laughed. "You really are going to have to give up this schoolboy crush. I've been nothing but a bitch to you since day one."

He grasped her hand and she looked at him in surprise. "I haven't been a boy in a long time, babydoll. And I'm more than man enough to deal with you and your so-called bitchiness."

She wished her body hadn't heard those words. The second he uttered *more than man enough*, her nipples went on red alert and she was a bit worried about the sudden dampness in her panties. She tried to tug her hand out of his grip, but he refused to relinquish it. "Listen, hotshot—"

"Save it, Nat. Why are you depressed?"

She panicked at his words. "I'm not depressed. I don't get depressed. *Ever.*" Her words came out far too loud and she watched him study her face intently. She bit her lower lip, realizing Ewan Collins was far too observant when it came to her. He was also cutting too close to the core. Honesty seemed her best bet. "I'm thirty-four years old and I have fuck-all to show for my life."

Ewan frowned. "That's not true. You own and operate an incredibly successful photography studio in Palm Springs. You're one of the most talented photographers I've ever met. Your pictures are beautiful."

She was taken aback by his praise, surprised he'd seen enough of her work to judge. "How do you know that?"

"I check out your website on occasion, plus Teagan is always emailing us pictures you've taken of her and Sky. You have an amazing eye."

"Yeah, that's me. The queen of composition, lighting, shading. Sometimes I feel like I've spent my entire life behind the lens of a camera."

Ewan lightly caressed the skin on the back of her neck and she marveled at how comforting the simple gesture was. "You sound like you're questioning your career choice."

"Do I?" she asked. "That's not my intention. I love my job. But sometimes I feel like that's all there is to me. I'm defined by a freaking camera."

"That's not true. I know Sky and Teagan consider you their friend, not their photographer."

"I know that. It's just..." She paused, trying to find a way to express the dark thoughts that had been plaguing her since her birthday. "It's just...*I'm* never in any of the pictures."

His eyebrows creased and she knew he was confused by her comment. She tried to clarify. "I'm not really sure what I have to show for my life. Hell, I'm not sure I've *lived* a life. I stand on the sidelines of every event, snapping picture after picture of other people living, celebrating, doing something. God, doing anything." Her voice betrayed her frustration and she took a breath, tried to calm down when she noticed Tris Collins glance up at her from the bar.

Ewan rubbed her hand, his other arm still draped around her, and she felt wholly surrounded by his presence. "What did you hope to have achieved by now that you haven't?"

His question caught her off-guard. She'd spent months commiserating over her lost youth, never once thinking about what it was she was grieving. And with one simple question, Ewan had thrown her for a loop…again. "Well, I don't know exactly. I've been to hundreds of weddings, birthday parties, bar mitzvahs, anniversaries. I've seen thousands of people celebrating events with loved ones. I've never done anything worth celebrating and even if I did, I wouldn't have anybody to commemorate it with. I know this may come as a surprise to you, but I don't generally have one of those personalities people flock to."

"Prickly?" he asked, though she knew his comment wasn't a question.

"No, not prickly. Strong-willed, self-assured, independent." She struggled to find those three words.

"Opinionated, arrogant, bitchy. Got it."

She opened her mouth to lambaste him and then closed it again. He was right. There was no debating the truth.

"Damn," he muttered. "You *are* down and out. No snappy comeback, Nat?"

She shook her head.

"I sort of got the impression you were happy on your own. You always say people are an annoyance you don't have time for."

She looked around the room briefly, wondering how she always got into these conversations with Ewan. He always made her say too much, tell too many secrets she never intended to reveal. "That's true. I guess maybe sometimes I think it might be nice to have a friend. Someone normal and not obnoxious. Someone who doesn't get their feelings easily hurt when I tell them they suck."

He laughed and she realized her requirements for a friend *did* sound pretty pathetic. "Isn't that Sky?" he asked.

"It was—I mean, is. It's just, he's got Teagan now and, well…things are different."

Ewan smiled and she felt a flash of anger spark. Here she was unloading all her misery, confessing things she'd never told another living soul, and he was giving her that stupid, annoying, lopsided grin.

She scowled. "Glad you find this all so funny. Get away from my table."

He moved closer and she fought to hold on to her annoyance. God, men as handsome as Ewan Collins should be illegal.

"I'm not laughing at you, babydoll. I'm just glad your problem is so easily solved."

She looked at him, confused. She'd spent months

feeling sorry for herself, trying to find a way out of her funk, and nothing had presented itself. Even leaving town for a change of scenery, a change of company hadn't helped.

She studied Ewan's confident face and realized that if anyone could solve her problem, it was probably him. Why she felt that way, she couldn't say. There was simply something deep inside her that said *trust him*.

"Show me the way." Her request was softly spoken, but Ewan heard it.

"How long are you staying here?" he asked.

"A week." It was Saturday afternoon and she had a flight booked to return to Palm Springs early in the morning the following Saturday.

Ewan rubbed his chin thoughtfully. "Seven days. It's a little tight, but we can manage."

"Manage what?"

"I'm going to teach you a lesson a day. Seven lessons you can live by so you never feel this way again. You, Natalie Miller, are about to get a life."

"Seven lessons? In seven days? And I'm going to learn *what*, exactly?"

"I'm going to show you all the stuff you've been missing out on while hiding behind the camera."

"I'm not sure this is such a good idea. I mean, I'm sort of here to help Teagan get ready for the wedding."

"Keira's already got a million plans for Teagan's wedding. She's in good hands, believe me. I'm serious about this, Natalie, but in order for it to work, you have to promise to follow through with the lessons. All of them. No backing out halfway. Promise?"

She considered his offer. Curiosity at what he had in mind was quickly overcoming common sense. Plus, the idea of spending seven days with Ewan was more appealing than she cared to admit.

Before she could reconsider or think too hard, she said, "Okay, I promise. You have seven days to show me what I've been missing."

"And you won't back out." She wondered why he kept stressing that part. What the hell did he have in mind?

"You have my word. I don't break promises."

"I believe you. Hey, Riley." Ewan called his younger sister over.

"What's up?" Riley asked.

"You going out tonight?"

"Do bees bee? Do bears bear?"

"How about letting me and Nat tag along? She's only here for a week so I thought we could show her some of the nightlife Baltimore has to offer."

Natalie could see Riley was shocked by Ewan's request. "You wanna go out with me?"

Ewan nodded.

Riley considered it. "Sure. Why not? Might be fun. But just so you know, you gotta hang. No bailing early."

"We won't bail."

"And I'm tramping it up," Riley added.

Ewan groaned as Natalie struggled to understand the conversation. "Tramping it up?"

Ewan looked at her and she could see he was amused by his sister's comments, though trying hard to look annoyed. "She means she's gonna go out looking like a hooker."

"I mean," Riley interrupted, "we're leaving by the fire escape."

"Why would you do that?" Natalie asked.

"Because I don't want to get a lot of grief from my brothers and Pop about my outfit. It's easier to just leave the apartment by the fire escape. No hassles, no dirty looks. That shit can really start the night out on a bad note." Riley studied Natalie's no-nonsense outfit and ponytail. "Meet me in the bathroom upstairs at eight-fifteen. You're gonna tramp it up too."

"Oh, that's okay. I don't really think—"

"She'll be there," Ewan replied with a mischievous grin. "I mean, we gotta hang, not bail." He mimicked his sister's words and Riley pulled his hair to show her annoyance.

"Very funny, shithead. I'll grab Aaron and see if he wants to come along."

"In other words, be your DD," Ewan said.

"Gotta be some perks to having a best friend who's a cop and overall do-gooder," Riley giggled before heading toward the bar to talk to Aaron.

"Me *tramping it up* is your first lesson on life?"

"We'll discuss what you learned after we go clubbing. Don't look so worried, Nat. This will be fun."

Fun. Yeah, right.

Because she was *so* good at fun. Not.

## CHAPTER TWO

S aturday Night…
Natalie grinned at something Riley said, responding in a voice too quiet for Ewan to hear, but Riley seemed to appreciate the comment as the two women burst into peals of laughter. It had been this way all night, starting with the ladies' hour-long makeup session in the bathroom.

He was glad to see Natalie relaxing, letting herself go. They'd gone out for a very late dinner before embarking on what Riley called her Saturday Night Special. His sister certainly knew how to have a good time. She'd regaled them with her over-the-top stories most of the evening and Ewan enjoyed seeing the constant smile on Nat's face.

Natalie pulled a small camera from her purse and started to take a picture, but Ewan confiscated it quickly. "You're off-duty. Remember?" He pocketed the camera, pleased when she merely rolled her eyes good-naturedly.

"You're in charge," she said.

He gazed at her, checking her out yet again and trying not to leer. He'd always considered himself a fan of natural beauty, but a tiny part of him found the "tramped-up" version of Natalie Miller hotter than hell. Her blonde hair, usually tied back in a tight pony-tail, was hanging loose and messy in an I-just-had-sex way. Reminded him of the pin-up girls from the dirty magazines he'd hidden under his mattress in middle school. Riley had done something magical to Nat's light blue eyes, lining them with black and covering the lids with a smoky gray color that made her look like one of those eighties models who lounged on the hood of a car while White Snake belted out tunes.

Natalie pushed her hair back as she and Riley talked and he was treated to a non-obstructed view of her breasts once again. She was in a sequined tank top and Riley had loaned her a barely there leather skirt that Ewan could *barely* keep his eyes off. She was fucking gorgeous and his cock had been locked in mortal combat with his jeans since they'd left the apart-ment via the fire escape. He wasn't entirely sure the denim was going to be strong enough to cage the monster for much longer.

This was their third club and a quick glance at his watch confirmed it was nearly two in the morning. His sister sure as hell knew her way around the nightclub scene. He was sure that would bug the shit out of him tomorrow when he *wasn't* well on his way to being three sheets to the wind.

He felt another elbow in his back as a drunk stumbled into his chair.

Aaron sent him a sympathetic look. "It's really crowded tonight."

"I didn't realize this many people lived in Baltimore," Ewan joked, although it did feel as if the entire population of the city was crammed within the four walls of the dingy club.

Aaron chuckled. "I'm a cop. Trust me. This isn't even one percent of the drunken lunatics who live around here."

"Okay, everybody ready?" Riley yelled, fighting to be heard over the ear-piercing music. Aaron gestured at Riley with his hand and Ewan laughed. Drunken lunatic was probably an apt description of his pixie of a sister. She passed around limes as she spoke and Ewan marveled that she willingly subjected herself to this torture every Saturday night—all in the name of fun.

"One, two, three!" At Riley's prompt, he licked the salt off his hand, drained the shot of tequila and popped the lime in his mouth. He grinned as Natalie winced.

"Fuck that burns." She wiped her mouth off with the back of her hand and shook her head, looking at him. "Tell me again why we're here?"

He had to fight back the grin at her monotone question. He wasn't quite sure why he got such a kick out of her sarcastic wit, but one of the reasons he enjoyed her company so much was simply because she made him laugh.

"We're here to have fun." He had to practically shout in her ear to make sure she could hear him.

"Ah. Be sure to let me know when that fun shit starts. Okay?"

He laughed. "Liar. You're having fun and you know it."

She shrugged noncommittally but her eyes, as always, told him the truth.

"Another round." Riley placed yet another lime in front of everyone except Aaron—who, as designated driver, was sipping on a Coke. Ewan wondered where his tiny sister was putting it all. This was their fourth shot each since arriving at this particular club. At the others, they'd merely consumed a couple beers each. "Laying a base," as Riley called it. Ewan had a feeling this wasn't going to end well. He never drank this much.

At the last minute he remembered the camera and handed it to Aaron, who took it as Riley waved the waitress over to set them up with another round of tequila.

"Last one, Riley," Aaron said. Riley rolled her eyes, but Ewan suspected that of everyone at the table, Aaron was the only person she'd actually listen to.

They went through the ritual one more time, each of them slamming their glasses down as Aaron snapped a picture.

Natalie looked at Ewan, blinking rapidly. "Should I be worried that I can't feel my lips anymore?"

Ewan grinned. "They're still there. Want me to try to kiss some feeling back into them?"

Natalie started to lean forward and Ewan felt like pumping a fist in the air in victory.

"Oh my God!" Riley shouted. "I love this song. Let's go dance." His sister grabbed Natalie before he could make good on his offer and Ewan sighed.

Aaron patted him on the back sympathetically. "Welcome to my weekends."

"How do you do this week in and week out?" Ewan was suddenly eyeing Riley's friend with a newfound respect.

Aaron shrugged. "I've done this so often with Riley, I'm starting to think it's normal, and God help me, even a little bit fun."

Ewan shook his head. "That's not good. You know that's not good, right?"

"Come on." Aaron pointed toward the dance floor. "You better go stake your claim. A woman as pretty as Natalie won't be alone for three seconds out on that dance floor before the wolves descend."

Even as Aaron spoke the words, Ewan could see two men moving closer, attempting to bump and grind their way into Riley and Natalie's dance space.

He pushed his way through the throng of dancers, taking Natalie's hand and pulling her away from the man whose hand had somehow managed to snake its way under the hem of her shirt, creeping ever steadily north. He narrowed his eyes when the man looked ready to protest that he'd robbed him of his new toy.

"Fuck off," Ewan mouthed. The man took his measure and then raised his hands in surrender, turning to thrust his hips against the woman behind him. Jesus. This place was meat market central. He was starting to wonder how he could get all of them out in one piece. The dimly lit dance floor was packed with sweaty, gyrating bodies all moving in time to the powerful bass thumping through the speakers only a few feet away from him. How much hearing loss was he going to suffer for this night?

Aaron quickly claimed Riley, pulling her farther into the horde. Natalie moved closer and Ewan saw she was relieved by his presence. He didn't bother to speak. No matter how loudly he yelled, the sound would only be consumed by the earsplitting music. He pulled her toward him, letting the music dictate his movements. The two of them swayed in time and he tried to calm his body's reaction when her hands wrapped around his waist, her hips lightly rasping his cock every few seconds.

Natalie seemed enraptured, lost in the music and the moment, and he fought back a groan when she turned around, pressing her ass against his dick and rubbing seductively in time to the beat.

"Fuck," he muttered, aware she couldn't hear his curse. There was no way she wouldn't be able to feel his hard-on through his jeans. Of course, given the amount of alcohol she'd consumed, he wondered if she minded. Her inhibitions were low, her resistance shot down by the tequila.

If he were a gentleman, he'd take her back to the table. Hell, he'd take her back to the apartment and tuck her into bed…alone. Instead, he grasped her waist and pulled her more firmly against him.

He wasn't a gentleman—and she felt too damn good.

Her hands drifted back, rubbing sensuously along his upper thighs, and he wrapped her tighter in his grip, letting his hands explore the tiny exposed bit of skin beneath her shirt, the same skin he'd just deprived the other guy of.

They continued to let the music take them away and Ewan felt for a moment as if he was having an out-of-body experience. The loud, thumping music matched the pulsating, relentless pumping of blood through his body. Natalie's hands as they caressed him seemed to leave a trail of fire wherever they touched, singeing him and driving him to heights he'd never imagined. She turned slowly in his arms and he felt as if her movements were in slow motion as the flashing, colored lights set the scene around them…the other dancers hazy, unreal. It was as if they were the only two people adrift in a sea of sound, touch, heat, light.

Natalie moved closer and he marveled that she could manage such a feat. He would have sworn they were already linked at every pleasurable point. Her stomach pressed against his cock while her hands traveled to his shoulders. He leaned down until their faces were connected—her soft cheek against his rough one, her hot breath tickling his ear. He turned slightly to kiss her flushed face—and she turned at the same time.

Their lips met.

He hadn't intended to kiss her, but Natalie affected him like season tickets to the Ravens affected his pop. He was helpless to resist.

Guided by the pure animal instincts she instilled within him, Ewan kissed her, their tongues tangling, and he tasted the same bitter tang of tequila that laced his own mouth. He moved his hands from her waist to her ass, pulling her ever closer, grinding against her swaying hips, and he felt her sigh against his lips.

Her fingers gripped his hair, tightening, holding his face to hers, their lips locked together. He could stay frozen in this moment and never leave, loving her soft sighs, her sensuous motions, her tantalizing touches. She was sex in heels and he wanted to eat her alive, soak up every glimmer of the beautiful radiance that shone from her face.

The moment was quickly ruined when a drunk girl fell down next to them, her drink splashing against their legs. While he barely felt it through his jeans, he saw Natalie shiver with the sudden cold drenching.

"Fuck," she mouthed as her eyes darted around the bar, panic written on her face. "Outside."

She went pale and he understood her distress, moving quickly to pull her off the dance floor and making a beeline for the first door he saw. They ended up in a back alley and Natalie quickly dashed to a Dumpster, bending over and gasping for air. He knew she was trying to stave off sickness.

"Might be better if you just let it out."

"Oh God, hate getting sick. Can't get sick. Can't get sick," she muttered, sucking in deep breaths, her words sounding like a mantra.

Dammit. She was drunk and he'd been an asshole, mauling her on the dance floor.

"Natalie." He took a step closer, but she waved him away.

"Please go away. I don't want you to see me like this."

He looked around. They were in a deserted alley behind a nightclub in the middle of the night. He wasn't going anywhere. Her pride be damned.

Trying to set her at ease, he stepped beside her. "I'm one of seven kids, Nat. Flu bugs were deadly when they hit our house. Little vomit's not gonna bother me."

She expelled a long breath and straightened up, leaning against the wall of the club. "I think I'm okay now. It was just the heat in there. It sort of got to me."

Sure, it was the heat. Had nothing to do with the tequila shots. He grinned and she scowled.

"How did I let you talk me into this? I'm too old for this shit."

"No, you're not."

Aaron appeared at the door. "Everything okay out here? I saw you guys leave, thought I'd better check on you."

"Natalie got a little overheated. Actually, I think maybe we should take off."

Aaron looked over his shoulder, back at the dance floor, and Ewan could read the concern on his face.

"I know Riley's not ready to leave. Why don't you stay with her and we'll catch a cab back to the pub?" Ewan suggested.

Aaron was obviously relieved. "Riley'd pitch a fit if we left now. It's still early."

Ewan rolled his eyes. Aaron really *had* spent too long with his sister if he thought two thirty was early. "Tell Riley I'm sorry we couldn't hang." He punctuated the word *hang* with air quotes and Aaron chuckled.

"No worries. I think she's surprised the two of you lasted this long. I'll get her home in one piece," Aaron promised.

"I know you will. Thanks, man. Tonight was fun." As he spoke the words, he realized they were true. Riley's life-of-the-party personality and Aaron's easygoing nature made them great companions and Ewan was suddenly sorry he hadn't taken them up on more of their offers to join them. He did tend to be a bit of a homebody. Or a fuddy-duddy, as Riley called him.

"Later." Aaron grinned before heading back inside.

"You think you can make it to the front curb, Nat? I'm gonna wave down a cab."

Natalie had listened to his conversation with Aaron silently. He could see her bout of nausea had disappeared and while she was clearly tipsy, she seemed steadier. Maybe it *had* been the heat.

"Tonight *was* fun," she reiterated.

He looked at her, feeling slightly surprised at her admission. "I'm glad you thought so."

"You can dance."

He laughed at her comment, relieved she wasn't pissed off by his overtures. "I think what I was doing was closer to swaying than actual dancing."

She crooked a finger, beckoning him closer, and he walked over until he stood directly in front of her. "You're so fucking hot."

He tried to hide his grin, well aware she would never say any of this while sober. "I've been telling you that for years, babydoll," he teased. He needed to get her home and in her own bed before she said too much more. While her inhibitions were down tonight, he didn't think she'd like remembering this conversation tomorrow when her walls were erected once more.

"Kiss me again."

He wanted to taste her lips more than he wanted his next breath, but the cool evening air had gone a long way toward killing his buzz. He'd already taken advantage of her inebriation once tonight. He wouldn't make the same mistake again. "Oh, I'm gonna kiss you again. You can be sure of that. But not tonight. We need to get home." She looked as if she wanted to protest his refusal, but instead she took his proffered hand and followed him to the front of the club.

"I just don't get you."

Ewan laughed. "So you've said. There's nothing to get, Nat. I'm a normal, run-of-the-mill guy. Nothing special or different."

She shook her head. "That's not true." She didn't elaborate, but with just those three words, Ewan felt his chest swell with affection. What the fuck was it with this woman? She'd consumed his thoughts and fantasies for three years. She had a biting, cutting, sarcastic wit that most people found off-putting, but for the life of him, he couldn't figure out why the rest of the world didn't see what he saw.

He waved down a taxi and helped her into the back. On the ride home, she was quiet as she rested her head on his shoulder. He thought she'd fallen asleep but as the driver pulled up in front of the apartment, she lifted her head. He paid and they walked into the darkened pub hand in hand. She stopped by the bar and he turned to look at her.

"I like it here. This pub."

He smiled. "I like it too. It's home."

"I grew up in a mansion."

He paused, studying her face. Natalie had never offered any information regarding her childhood, though he'd tried to start the conversation a few times. "A mansion? Cool," he said casually.

"This bar, the apartment above. I would have given anything to grow up here. It's warm. So warm."

"Natalie?"

His question seemed to draw her out of her thoughts. "You gonna keep me up all night talking shit or can I try to get some sleep now?"

He grinned at the return of her caustic tone. "Oh, I'll get your ass to bed. No worries there, babydoll." He bent and swiftly picked her up in his arms, the way someone would carry a newborn baby.

"What the—" Her words were drowned out by her drunken laughter as he carried her up two flights of stairs. Instinctively, her arms wrapped around his neck. He knew if she'd been sober she'd have been pissed as hell, but when he dumped her unceremoniously in the middle of the bed, she was still giggling.

"Now…" He bent over her on the bed and silently rejoiced when her laughter turned to a breathless gasp. "Bedtime, angel."

She shook her head. "I'm no angel. Satan's spawn, if my colleagues are to be believed."

He cupped her cheek with his hand. "You're the sweetest angel on earth." He meant his words as a compliment, but she burst into laughter again and soon he found himself joining her.

"Jesus, *that* was corny," she teased.

He rolled his eyes. "You know what your problem is?"

She shook her head.

"You have no romance in your soul."

Natalie struggled to stop laughing. "If I fell for that *sweetest angel* crap, would that make me romantic?"

He scowled, though he felt no anger. "It wouldn't hurt you to try."

"I think I'd rather be called," she paused thought-fully, "babydoll. Even if it *is* sexist as shit."

He grinned. "Told you that you liked that nickname."

"I like it better than that *sweetest angel on earth* dribble."

He joined her laughter this time. "Goodnight, Nat," he said, bending down to kiss her nose playfully.

"Wait. I'm stuck."

"Stuck?"

"In this fucking skirt your sister painted on me. Help me?"

He sucked in a painful breath. "I don't think—"

"Please?"

He could see she was still under the affects of the alcohol and this fallen angel was definitely trying to tempt him toward certain purgatory.

He swallowed heavily, trying to close his mind to the next few minutes. "Pull back the covers," he instructed. If he was going to help her get undressed, he was going to make sure there was something on hand to hide her with.

She crawled under the sheets, lying on her back patiently with a heavy-lidded look that proved she knew what she was doing. He pulled down he tab of the side zipper on her leather skirt. She raised her hips off the bed and he grimaced at the fresh surge of blood the movement sent to his cock.

"Fuck," he whispered when she grinned and started shimmying the leather down her hips. She wasn't kidding about the tight fit. He helped her work the material over her hips, pulling it free of her legs. For three seconds he stared, spellbound at the sight of her bare thighs and the tiny bit of lace covering her—

He pulled the covers over her body, turning quickly.

"So what was my lesson?" she asked.

He struggled to find the breath to speak. He kept his back turned. "What do you think? What did you learn?"

She considered his question and he silently prayed

he hadn't fallen short. It was just his first lesson. He had six more days to convince Natalie that life was worth living. If she would simply open the door to new experiences and all the people she generally kept at arm's length, she could have a full, amazing life.

"I think you wanted me to have fun. Loosen up?"

He turned to face her, grinning. "That was it. You said you had fun. Did you mean it?"

She graced him with a genuine smile. "I did. I really did. Your sister's a hoot. My kind of sarcastic bitch."

He stepped closer, relieved she was still buried beneath the covers. He bent down to tuck her in. "Yeah, that's Riley all right. There's nothing wrong with letting go, Nat. Laughing, drinking tequila, doing a little dirty dancing. It's all harmless fun."

She touched his cheek and he swallowed back the desire to move even closer. "You're a good teacher, Ewan."

He savored the sound of his name on her lips, wondering if he'd ever heard her say it. In the past, he'd always been hotshot, kiddo. Never Ewan.

"Night, Nat." He had to leave while the getting was still good. He wanted far too much from Natalie Miller. Needed too much.

"Wait," she called out. He was nearly to the door. Four more steps and he'd be free. Free to hit the shower—a cold one. Free to jerk himself off—a lonely one.

"You said you'd kiss me."

He closed his eyes and prayed for strength.

"Tomorrow, Nat. I'll kiss the shit out of you tomorrow. Not tonight. Don't ask me."

She fell silent and he wondered if she'd passed out. He turned slowly, surprised to find her sitting up, staring at him.

"I just don't get you," she whispered.

"You will, babydoll. Soon."

# CHAPTER THREE

Sunday…

"Nat. Natalie."

She opened her eyes, squinting against the bright light shining on her face. It took several painful blinks before she could focus on Ewan's face.

"Get lost," she muttered, closing her eyes against his far too cheerful face. Her head felt as if it was about to split apart and her mouth was too dry to say more than the two words she'd already uttered.

"I was afraid you wouldn't feel well," he whispered. "Listen. I've brought you a glass of water and a couple aspirin. I need you to sit up and take them. We're on a tight schedule or else I'd let you sleep this off some more."

She tried to open her eyes again but the effort was simply too difficult. "What the fuck are you talking about?"

"We're going out. In an hour. I need you to take

these pills, then get up and get a shower. It will help, trust me."

"I'm not going anywhere."

"You gave me seven days, Nat. Seven lessons. You agreed."

"It's freaking dawn." Her voice was shrill and she winced at the pain the sound of her own voice caused. "Jesus, what kind of masochist are you?" She gripped her head.

"It's eleven o'clock, babydoll. That's hardly dawn. Now get up."

She opened her eyes and pierced him with a glare that had destroyed stronger men than Ewan Collins. He merely stared her down. "Now, Nat. I don't want to have to dump a bucket of cold water on you, but I will."

"I will crush you like a bug if you try it." She tried to invoke as much threatening menace into her voice as possible, but for some reason her powers of evil didn't work against the idiot and he laughed.

"Come on. I've planned a nice day for you. I don't want you to miss it."

"What are we doing?" she asked.

"Fishing. With Pop."

"On the shore or on a boat?" The thought of getting on anything that rocked suddenly sent her stomach into lurch mode and she swallowed heavily.

"Boat, but it'll be a gentle ride. Take the aspirin. Get a shower. You'll feel better. I promise."

She sat up gingerly, ready to be assaulted by a mammoth head rush. She was pleasantly surprised when it didn't come. She rubbed her eyes, unaware of Ewan's sudden silence until she opened them again and looked at his stunned expression.

His line of vision had drifted somewhat south of her neck and she glanced down. She was naked, the sheets hovering around her waist, giving her male friend more than an eyeful of her naked breasts.

"Shit," she muttered, quickly pulling the sheets around her. "Where are my pajamas?"

"I didn't take your *shirt* off last night, I swear."

His oddly worded reply caught her attention and she lifted the sheets, shielding her body from his sight. Sure enough, her skirt was missing as well. "What part of my clothing *did* you take off?"

He crossed his arms across his chest smugly. "I didn't take off anything you didn't ask me to."

She gritted her teeth, fighting to remember the previous night. She had definite flashes of memory, though none of them were things she wanted to focus on too much. "You can leave now. I'm up."

"So am I," he joked, wiggling his eyebrows suggestively and she laughed, the action sending another slash of pain through her head.

"Don't make me laugh. Go away, you pervert. I'll be downstairs in a minute."

He chuckled and left her alone with her thoughts. Fishing? With his pop? Oh hell. How did she get herself in to this mess? She'd never been fishing in her life. She'd never *wanted* to go fishing. If she made a bucket list right now, fishing would be at the very bottom, along with turkey hunting and attending a NASCAR race.

She sighed as she considered the previous night's activities. She hadn't wanted to go clubbing with Riley either, now that she thought about it, and despite the fact she was suffering, she'd had a really good time. She picked up the glass and swallowed the two aspirin Ewan had thoughtfully supplied—and then it hit her.

She'd slept all night. Slept peacefully for nearly eight hours.

Passed out was probably more the truth, but she didn't care. She'd slept a full night.

*Hot damn.*

Maybe playing along with Ewan's experiment would pay off in ways she hadn't foreseen. If she ignored her throbbing head, she was actually well rested and… She tried to find the words to describe her state. Less heavy was all that came to her.

She felt *lighter* this morning.

TWO HOURS LATER, she found herself standing on the bank of a lake waiting for Pat's friend to drop his bass boat into the water—and feeling a return of her usual irritability and impatience. They'd driven over an hour to get to this bug-infested pond to ride around in a boat that was older than she was, and now they were supposed to try to catch a bunch of stinky fish. She hated fish. Never ate it. Shrimp and crab legs slathered in butter were her usual fare at a seafood restaurant.

She suspected they wouldn't be finding any of those in this murky brown water.

Oh yeah, this was a good idea.

"Can we just pretend we did this and go home? I'd kill for a nap."

Ewan stepped closer to her, gave her that sweet grin she was starting to find endearing. "Come on, babydoll. Give it a chance."

"Whoa!" she burst out when it looked like the man with the boat was going to drive his trailer and truck right into the lake.

Ewan put his arm around her. "It's okay, Nat. The boat launch goes down quite a ways."

"My head hurts," she murmured, pushing her sunglasses up in an attempt to shield her sensitive eyes from the bright rays slicing into her brain like a laser.

"Today won't be hard. Promise."

"You said that about last night." She shrugged off his arm as she spoke, trying to express her annoyance at being dragged out of her bed far too early after their very late night. Her willingness to give fishing a chance had ended when her headache didn't. "By the way, I'm never drinking tequila again. If that's on any more of your so-called life lesson plans, mark it off now."

Ewan grinned. "That's one vow I'm willing to take with you. My head feels like it's going to split apart."

She looked up, surprised by his admission. "You didn't tell me you felt bad too."

"You were bitching enough for both of us."

She scowled, and then realized he was right. "I told you I was bitchy. Gave you ample warning. I guess you're reconsidering this whole seven-day deal, aren't you?"

He shook his head. "You haven't figured it out yet, have you, Nat?"

"Figured out what?"

"I like you. Just you. The way you are." He paused to let his words soak in and Nat felt uncharacteristic warmth build in her chest. He liked her.

No one liked her.

Then he added, "Even if you *are* a gigantic pain in the ass."

She giggled. "Want some aspirin? I brought along the bottle."

"I took a couple at home. Besides, I have a feeling a few minutes on the water will be more than enough to cure my aches and pains." He pulled her in front of him so her back rested against his chest, wrapping his arms loosely around her waist and placing his chin on top of her head. She leaned back, letting him envelop her, marveling at how much warmth he could put into a simple embrace.

She watched his pop help his friend offload the boat for a few minutes. "Shouldn't we help?" she asked.

"I offered, but Pop said I'd only be in the way. These guys have been coming to this lake once a month for nearly twenty years. They've got their routine down to an art form. Besides, it looks like they're ready."

"Damn," Pop said, walking over to them. "Hate that we're getting such a late start."

"Late start?" she muttered, realizing their tardiness was her fault. "Sorry."

Ewan gave her a quick squeeze. "No worries, Nat. Pop would have been complaining about being late even if he'd been out here at daybreak."

Pat grinned. "Never too early to get out on that water."

The older man with the truck finished tying the boat to the pier and walked over to greet them. Natalie thought he appeared to be about the same age as Ewan's father, though Pat had aged a bit better than his friend, who was totally bald and supporting at least two spare tires around his middle. He was dressed in head-to-toe camouflage and the word *redneck* briefly floated through her city-girl mind.

"Well hello, Ewan. Long time, no see," he said, shaking hands with Ewan. "I was glad to hear you were joining us this weekend. And who is this pretty lady?"

Ewan did the introductions. "Moose, this is Natalie Miller, a friend from California. Nat, this is Moose."

Moose gripped her hand, shaking it firmly.

"Please God, tell me Moose is *not* your given name."

The man laughed, albeit a bit too loudly for Natalie, who fought not to wince at the sound. "Nah. It's a nickname, but I probably shouldn't share how I got it in mixed company. Not polite."

Natalie blushed, but Pat just shook his head, laughing. "Sweet Mary, you've been trying to pass that lie off as the truth for forty years."

"Maybe one of these years it'll stick," Moose said.

Natalie narrowed her eyes playfully, feigning anger at being taken in by his crude joke. "You hunt for moose?" she asked, thinking he certainly looked the part.

"His last name is Moosefield," Ewan explained.

"Ah." She grinned and shook her head. "Well, that's certainly a letdown. Shame on you, Moose."

"You were thinking something really naughty, weren't you, sweet stuff?" Moose teased, enjoying having a bit of fun at her expense.

It was a shame he'd just met his match. "Nope, not really. But then I know how you fishermen are with your fish tales." She held her hands up, as if she were measuring something a couple feet long, before slowly drawing them together until there was only an inch or two between her palms.

Pat hooted with laughter. "Hee hee! She's got your number, old boy. Good girl, Natalie."

Moose guffawed loudly before grasping her hand. "Come on and get in this boat, sweet stuff. This is gonna be fun. I bet I make a real fisherman outta you and before the day is through, you'll be telling some fish tales of your own."

Ewan and Pat followed them aboard the boat. They all took a seat and Natalie relaxed as Moose took them for a cruise farther out onto the lake. They pulled back in close to shore before Moose cut the engine. According to Pat, they'd arrived at their world famous fishing spot.

"World famous, eh?" she asked. "Funny. I don't see any paparazzi hovering on the shoreline."

Moose laughed. "That's because it's a super-secret spot."

"How do you know you can trust me not to divulge the location?"

Pat looked at her with a crooked grin, acting as if he'd just realized their mistake. "I knew we should have blindfolded her. You said we could trust her, Ewan."

Ewan looked at her with mock seriousness. "I did vouch for your upstanding character, Nat."

"You lied to your father?" she asked. "Pretty sure you go to hell for that, hotshot."

Moose came over and slapped her on the shoulder. "I like this gal. She's got spirit. Come on now. We need to get organized. The fish aren't gonna hop in the boat."

"They aren't?" she asked, only partly joking. "Shit."

The men started assembling assorted equipment and Natalie marveled over the tremendous amount of stuff needed for fishing. And here she thought she had a lot of photography equipment. Ewan had returned her small digital camera this morning and she pulled it from her backpack to snap a few pictures of Ewan and his pop and Moose.

Ewan caught her and took the camera again. "Strike two, babydoll. I can see I'm going to have to hold on to this camera until you leave next weekend. You're off-duty. Today is about fishing, not photography."

He handed her a pole. "Great," she said, failing to mask her lack of enthusiasm. "A fishing pole. Just what I've always wanted. You sure do know the way to a girl's heart."

"Did you just call that a pole?" Moose asked.

Natalie nodded. "I know I've never been fishing before, but I can tell a fishing pole when I see one."

"You've never been fishing?" Moose's questions were becoming more aghast by the minute. "Sweet stuff. Number one, that's a fishing *rod*. And number two, where the hell is your father? Why didn't he take you fishing?"

Natalie rolled her eyes at his rod comment. "Semantics. Rod, pole, whatever."

Ewan smirked. "It's a rod. He and Pop are purists when it comes to that."

"Fine. Thank you for letting me use your fishing *rod* today and my dad was a workaholic. It's sort of hard to take your daughters fishing when you work twenty-four-seven."

"What about your mother?" Moose asked.

Natalie laughed. "The alcoholic June Cleaver? Um, no. Fishing doesn't seem to be one of those sports you can do in pearls with a gin and tonic in your hand."

The men fell silent and Natalie cursed herself for her too-revealing, too rude comments about her parents. She decided a change of subject was her only shot at trying to salvage the mood she'd just killed. "So I suppose I just put this hook in the water and wait?"

Ewan laughed and Moose shook his head. "Ah, Natalie. Come over here, sweet stuff. You let Uncle Moose teach you all about fishing."

She rolled her eyes. "Uncle Moose? You do realize I'm thirty-four years old."

"Doesn't matter how old you are. Sounds to me like

you need an adult male influence to teach you the finer things in life. Like fishing."

"Fishing is a finer thing?"

"It's the best thing."

He reached down and grabbed a Styrofoam cup full of dirt. "You need to put bait—in this case, a night crawler—on your hook, and then you cast it into the water."

She glanced at the cup. "Fine, Uncle Moose. How about you dig around in that dirt and bait my hook for me because there's no way I'm touching a worm. I just got a manicure." She flashed her freshly painted nails at him, but the men didn't seem deterred.

Pat rubbed the back of his neck and stepped closer. "Well, Natalie, I'm afraid on this boat, it's every man for himself. Go on and dig in there and get yourself a nice, fat worm. They don't bite."

She blew out a deep breath and then reached into the cup, wrinkling her nose as she pulled out a worm. It wiggled and she dropped it. "It's still alive!"

Moose laughed and bent down to pick up her squirming bait. "Of course it is. What did you think?"

"I thought it would be a dead worm."

Moose shook his head. "Here, I'll show you how to do it this first time." He grasped her hook and deftly poked in through the worm several times. "There you go. Next time, you do it just like that."

She looked around at the men, her gaze freezing when she caught Ewan's amused smirk. "That's disgusting."

"That's fishing, babydoll. Come here. I'll show you

how to cast." She crossed to the other side of the boat as Moose and Pat prepared their own rods. Ewan stood behind her, showing her the finer points of casting her line successfully. Once she had her hook in the water, Ewan followed suit with his own.

"Now what?" she asked.

"Now, we wait. If that bobber goes under the surface, you've got a bite and that's when you want to reel it in. Until then, we sit down and relax."

They both claimed a chair. Glancing over her shoulder, she could see Pat and Moose had done the same, the two old friends settling into a quiet conversation.

"How long do we have to wait?" she asked after watching her bobber float for several minutes.

"Who knows? Could be five minutes or five hours or not at all."

"Not at all? Are you seriously telling me we're going to wait for hours even if we aren't catching anything?"

Ewan nodded. "That's just fishing, Nat. Some days are diamonds, some are stone."

"You expect me to sit here for hours on end watching that little ball float on the water? Where's the fun in that?"

"Close your eyes," Ewan prompted.

"I thought I was supposed to watch the bobber."

"Close your eyes, smartass."

She obeyed after rolling said eyes. "They're closed."

"Now listen," Ewan said, his voice soft. "Listen to the light slapping of the water against the side of the boat. Listen to the birds singing. Feel the gentle sway, rocking you like a mother rocks her baby. Feel that warm breeze as it strokes your face. Take a deep breath of that sweet, fresh air, Nat. Let if fill up your lungs and clean out all the dark, dirty worries creeping around inside you." After each direction he paused for several moments, letting her do exactly as he suggested.

She listened to his words, letting the sounds, the smells, the feelings fill her up until she felt as if she were asleep, though wide awake.

"How do you feel?" he asked.

"Relaxed. Peaceful." Boneless, content, comfortable, calm. A multitude of words flowed through her mind—each one more gentle, more soothing than the one before. She felt…good.

Ewan's hand lightly stroked the skin at the back of her neck. "Now open your eyes and watch the bobber. It's not a difficult thing to do, so while you do it, you can let your mind wander. Let it go. Why not enjoy the scenery? There's a heron over there on the shore. See it?"

"Yes."

They sat together in quiet contentment for nearly half an hour. Slowly reeling in their bait, only to cast it out again. She listened to Pat and Moose talk about family and work and past fishing trips as she studied the quiet serenity of their surroundings. None of them had had so much as a nibble, but she could see the attraction of the outing. No wonder Moose and Pat looked forward to this day each month.

"Nat," Ewan said, sitting up quickly. "You've got a bite."

She'd been so distracted by a flock of birds on the shore she'd forgotten to look at her bobber. "I do?"

The older men turned excitedly.

"Okay, here we go, sweet stuff," Moose instructed. "Reel him in nice and slow."

She followed his instructions, amazed by the strength of the fish on the other end of her line. "He must be huge," she said. "I can barely move this reel."

Ewan moved behind her, placing his hands on her waist but letting her do the work. He whispered directions and praise as she continued to pull the fish in. Finally Moose bent over the side of the boat with a net as she lifted her rod. A gleaming silver fish floundered in the net as Moose lifted him into the boat.

"Well, will you look at that," Pat said. "That's not a bad effort for your first time fishing."

"Not a bad effort?" she repeated. "That fish is huge!"

Pat and Moose laughed while they worked together to pull the hook out of the fish's mouth.

"Fish tales," Moose muttered, but she wasn't dissuaded from her opinion. He was just jealous, she thought with a delighted grin.

Moose held the wriggling fish out to her and curiosity drove her toward it. She took a deep breath and reached out to touch it.

"You'll have to do better than that. It's your fish. You have to kiss it."

She narrowed her eyes at the older man. "I'm not kissing that fish."

"Rules of the boat," Pat interjected. "You wouldn't

want to offend your captain. It's a tradition—we always kiss our fish. You better be quick though, that poor guy can't stay out of the water much longer."

"You're throwing him back?" she asked, struggling to understand the purpose of fishing if you didn't keep what you caught.

"This is a catch-and-release trip," Moose replied. "Now pucker up and give this poor little guy some love. Bound to be traumatized after having that hook in his mouth."

She bent forward, amazed by the realization she was actually going to kiss a fish. She placed a peck on the scaly, cold thing as Pat and Moose howled with laughter.

Moose released the fish back into the lake and Natalie had an anxious moment as she wondered if she'd killed the poor thing. Her fear was short-lived as the fish quickly swam away.

She wiped her mouth off with the back of her hand, narrowing her eyes at the two older men who were still chuckling. Realization dawned hard. "You never kiss the fish, do you?"

Moose tried to look remorseful but his attempt was spoiled by the shit-eating grin plastered on his face. "I didn't think you'd really do it."

She gave Ewan a dirty look when she caught him chuckling as well. "Don't look at *me*. It's every man for himself on the boat."

"So I keep hearing," she said. "Well, that's okay boys. Laugh it up. Because if I'm not mistaking, I'm the only one on this boat who's caught a fish *to* kiss."

Pat sobered up quickly. "Hey, now. That hurts."

She grinned as she reclaimed her rod, deftly baiting her hook and casting it with confidence. "Yep, looks like I'm kicking ass in the fishing game."

The other men laughed and she was surprised when Moose came over and playfully tugged on her ponytail. "Day's still young, sweet stuff."

She smiled at him and his words. The day was still young…and she hoped it lasted forever.

IT WAS NEARLY nine when Natalie descended the stairs, smiling at him as she approached the couch. Ewan was grateful for his loose sweatpants when she appeared in her plaid pajama bottoms and a T-shirt. They'd decided to watch a DVD together after they'd returned from fishing.

"Where's your pop?" she asked.

"Watching the sports channel in his bedroom. Twenty bucks says we hear him snoring in half an hour."

She laughed. "What about your sisters?"

"Teagan's spending the night with Keira and Riley's in her room sleeping off last night."

She sat down beside him and he quickly bent to grab her legs, pulling them over his lap as she lay against the armrest of the couch.

"Comfortable?" he asked.

"Mmm hmm."

He was taken aback again by her quietness tonight.

She'd taken to the fishing experiment better than he'd hoped and as the day passed, he'd watched her fall deeper and deeper into a state of total relaxation. It looked good on her.

He didn't realize before how sharp-eyed, focused and alert Natalie usually was. She was a bundle of nervous energy, never landing, never sitting for long.

They were nearly an hour into the movie when he felt her gaze on his face. He turned to look at her, confused by her expression.

"I shouldn't have said all that stuff about my parents. On the boat. It wasn't really the truth."

"Your dad isn't a workaholic?" He'd always wondered about her family, her childhood. It was the one subject she steadfastly refused to talk about.

"He is. He just wasn't always. He was a good dad, just not a fisherman."

Ewan grinned. "Not all men are, but don't tell Pop and Moose that. I have to admit I was curious about the June Cleaver comment."

"My mother lives her life looking absolutely perfect while sitting on a pristine white couch in an immaculate house. She loves the illusion of it, I suppose."

"And the gin?"

"A bottle a week, every week. More over the holidays. So much for perfection."

Ewan wanted to ask more, but he could see from the tightness around her eyes, she wouldn't go any further with this conversation than she already had.

"You said something about your dad never taking

his daughters fishing. I assume that means you have sisters?" he asked.

"Had a sister. Just one. She died in a car accident."

He could tell those words were being pulled from her with every ounce of strength she possessed and he knew he should let the subject stop there. "I'm sorry, Nat. My mom died of cancer when I was twelve. I don't think there are words to really describe…" His words fell away. He rarely talked about Sunday, his mother, to anyone—least of all his siblings.

He was worried they'd figure out how much he'd forgotten about her.

Sometimes he lay in bed and tried to force his memories of her to return, but most of the scenes he could recreate were made-up versions of the stories his older brothers and sisters liked to tell about their mother.

"You're right," she said softly, pulling him from his troubling thoughts. "There aren't words. So let's don't try."

He narrowed his eyes at her short response. Natalie could flash from red-hot to ice-cold in less than a millisecond. But in this instance, he wanted to change the subject as much as she did.

"Don't worry about what you said on the boat. The more you talked, the more apparent it became to those guys that it's just your way." He grinned as he spoke and she scowled.

"Is that your way of saying I'm cynical?"

He turned, lifting one of her legs and pulling it over his head until her legs were wrapped around his waist.

Her eyes darkened with desire and he felt the same wave knock him down as well. "Let's just say you're cynical with the right amount of romance."

She snorted, a genuine snort, and he laughed. "I think I missed the day they gave out romance."

"Haven't you ever been in love?" he asked, curious about her past relationships. He'd never heard Teagan or Sky mention Natalie having boyfriends or even dating.

"Well, I suppose I have."

"You suppose?"

"I've had boyfriends, Ewan. Done a bit of dating. Just not lately. Work keeps me busy and, well…there's that case of bitchiness we've discussed."

"Dating's not love, babydoll."

She looked at him, biting her lower lip. "Semantics," she said.

"So you've never been in love." His comment wasn't a question and she didn't bother to refute it.

"Too busy. Not interested. Men annoy me."

He laughed at her list, but decided to let her off the hook. He lowered to his elbows, trapping her beneath him on the couch. He could see her chest rise and fall as her breathing accelerated.

"What are you doing?" she asked.

"Time for a little pop quiz. What did you learn from today's lesson? One kiss for every right answer."

"A kiss?"

He kissed the end of her nose. "Just a kiss."

He watched myriad emotions fly across her face as she considered his offer and he wondered if she remembered kissing him on the dance floor last night. He was fairly certain she did. He'd caught her looking at him a few times today on the boat, a slight flush on her cheeks.

"I learned how to relax."

He bent forward to kiss her but she pressed her fingers to his lips before they could touch hers.

"I'm not sure this is a good idea," she said.

"Why not?" He wanted to move out of this just-friends hell she'd placed them in the past three years. He knew she didn't give a shit about their age difference but something was definitely holding her back, and if her earlier comments were true, that something wasn't simply keeping her from *him*, but from all men.

"There doesn't seem to be much point." Her answer was frustratingly vague and insulting, until he spotted the genuine panic in her eyes. She was scared.

He decided to pull back and put the kiss in terms she could accept—place it in a category that wouldn't make her uncomfortable with him. It was still early. He had time to wear her down. Not a lot of time, but some. "Does there have to be a point?"

"Doesn't there?"

He gave her a wolfish grin, hoping it would distract her from the truth. "I think making out on a couch is more relaxing than fishing."

"So this is still part of the lesson?" Her question proved she'd fallen for his ploy. A small grin crossed his face.

He gripped her cheeks in his hands. He wasn't stopping again. He'd ease her into it but he wouldn't be denied. Not when he could see obvious interest emerging.

"You ready to relax some more?" he asked.

She didn't answer. Instead she rose up slightly, meeting his lips halfway. Her hands flew to his hair and his intention of giving her a peck was washed away by her tongue, her sweet breath as they consumed each other in a flurry of hungry, no-holds-barred, open-mouthed kisses.

So much for her fear. It wasn't the affection, the touches holding her back. Natalie Miller was afraid of relationships. Commitment.

He filed the thought away for later. For several minutes, he let himself fall into the moment, into her. It was always this way whenever she was with him—he simply couldn't stop touching her, wanting her.

He pulled away, gentling her with soft kisses against her smooth cheeks. "What else did you learn today?"

Her heavy-lidded eyes looked at him and he wondered if she'd heard the question. "I learned I need to get out more often. Commune with nature, as it were."

"Good answer." He kissed her again, his hands drifting down to cup her breasts in his palms, testing her limits. She moaned against his mouth, pressing up into his grip. She wasn't wearing a bra.

He chuckled at the little voice telling him he was about to make it to second base in his family living room with his dad asleep in the next room. Christ, he really needed to get his own place.

"What's so funny?" she asked breathlessly.

"I haven't made out in this living room in years. I'm gonna steal second."

She laughed. "Oh hotshot. I wouldn't suggest it."

He tweaked her nipple firmly and she let out a little cry. "I'm not sure but I think the third-base coach is waving me on."

He rose until he was kneeling between her open legs. He grasped the hem of her T-shirt, slowly pushing it up. He half expected her to call a halt. Though they'd touched often over the past two days, he hadn't advanced their play to this extent. She watched him as he lifted her shirt above her breasts and he could tell she was holding her breath. One look at her bare chest and he felt his own breath leave in a rush.

His eyes glanced at her face as he moved closer. "You're beautiful."

"Kiss me," she whispered. He didn't have to be asked twice. He lightly took her breasts in his hands, his lips immediately engulfing her right nipple, sucking the pebbled tip into his mouth. She gasped and he knew he'd surprised her with his speedy assault. If he'd been able he would have teased her a bit first, but he was only human and he'd dreamed of this moment for years.

Her fingers threaded through his hair, tugging almost painfully as her legs wrapped around his waist. She was mindlessly gyrating against his stomach and he wondered if she'd been as long without sex as he had. He was starving for her, his finesse shot to hell by her needy response.

"Easy," he murmured against her flushed skin. "I know what you need and I'll give it to you."

He sucked her breast back into his mouth. With his free hand, he tweaked her other nipple, pinching it until she was squirming beneath him once more. He kissed his way across her breast, up her neck, until his lips rested at the shell of her ear. "I'm coming around to third. What's the call gonna be, Nat?"

He was a fool for giving her a choice. Her body, her flushed face, told him she was his for the taking, but he didn't want to seduce her into something she'd only regret in the morning. He wanted her with him in this —one hundred percent.

He dragged his hand along the smooth skin of her stomach, working his fingers under the elastic band at her waist slowly. "Make the call."

She stared at him for several painfully long moments. "You're out," she whispered.

He froze, his fingers resting lightly just above her pussy. "Out?"

She nodded slowly. "I think…I'm sure. Definitely out."

He pulled his hand away, brushing a stray hair away from her face. "I won't stop trying," he warned her. "I get three outs. This was only one."

She looked at him and he wished he could read what was going on in her mind. Her face wasn't telling him a thing. She wasn't smirking, wasn't giving him a cocky victorious look. If anything she looked sad, guilty, tired.

"I have to warn you," she said quietly. "I'm one helluva ballplayer."

He chuckled, hoping to coerce a smile from her, trying to bring back the lightheartedness he'd seen in her face all day. He pressed his erection into her stomach, grinning when she gasped. "That's sort of what I'm hoping for, Nat. I've actually got a couple of balls right here—"

She laughed, shoving at his shoulders, and he was relieved to see her spunky personality reemerge. "Get off me, you dirty boy. I'm going to bed. Alone."

He pushed away from her, rising as she did, watching as she pulled her shirt back down. She headed for the stairs but he stopped her, his hands grasping her waist.

"No cheating," he said.

She looked at him, confused, but before she could ask, he clarified. "No vibrator. You don't want me yet, that's fine, but don't you dare get yourself off with a piece of plastic, pretending it's me."

Her gaze narrowed and he braced himself for a fight. He wasn't sure why he'd started this battle after all the trouble he'd just gone through to lighten the mood again. All he knew was that he wouldn't be able to sleep tonight if he thought she was finding her release without him, retreating back into her safe, lifeless box. She wasn't going to take any more steps backward. From this moment on, they were moving forward.

"Another lesson?" Her question was laced with anger.

"I won't be used in a fantasy when you've rejected the real thing. It doesn't work that way."

She closed her eyes wearily. "Fine."

"Fine?"

She gave him a laugh, looking at him again and placing her palm against his cheek. "Seems a fair enough exchange. So long as the same deal applies to you." She looked down at his obvious erection. "Hands off."

He wanted to groan at the case of blue balls he was about to spend his night suffering through. "You are a cold, cold woman, Natalie Miller." He smiled as he spoke and she giggled.

"I warned you."

"So you did. And now I'm giving you a warning of your own. I'm gonna score in this game. I'm gonna score big."

She acknowledged the challenge with a wicked look before turning to climb the stairs. The word "maybe" drifted down as she reached the top and he sighed, looking down at his cock.

"Sorry," he muttered to the poor appendage. He chuckled as he walked to his own room. It was going to be a long night.

## CHAPTER FOUR

**M**onday…

"Come on, babydoll. Rise and shine."

Natalie opened her eyes to find Ewan leaning over her bed. "You have a nasty habit of waking me up too early in the morning. What do you say we try to break it? Right now. Before I break your nose."

She'd trudged up the stairs to Tristan's old bedroom after Ewan issued his demand and she'd spent half the night tossing and turning, trying to figure out what the hell she was doing. She'd only been in Baltimore three days and she was practically throwing herself at Ewan every other minute. He claimed their physical interactions were just part of the game they were playing, but she wasn't so sure. Sometimes when he looked at her…

Ewan, as usual, ignored her threat and kissed her forehead. Her stomach always did flip-flops whenever he pressed one of his platonic kisses to her face. She loved his little pecks on her nose, her cheeks, her brow, as much as his full-on, open-mouth, extravaganza-style kisses. "Time is money. I've brought your uniform up here. Thought you might want to try it on first."

"Uniform?"

"Well, actually it's just a Sunday's Side polo shirt. I brought you a ladies medium. Figured you might need a little extra room to contain the girls."

He followed his dirty joke with a quick leer at her breasts and she fought to restrain her laughter. It wouldn't do to encourage his bad behavior.

"Although in hindsight, I wouldn't have minded watching your pretty tits strain against a shirt that was just a bit too small all day either."

She held up her hand to ward off any more of his comments. "Okay, number one, *ew*. And number two, my *girls* are none of your concern and I suggest you focus your attention of what's residing above my neckline or you might find yourself with a crotch full of my knee. Got it?"

His mischievous grin proved he wasn't about to change his ways.

She gave him a dirty look. "Why would I want to wear a Sunday's Side shirt?"

"All the waitresses wear them with khaki pants." He suddenly looked concerned. "Do you have khaki pants in your luggage?"

"I think so, but I'm not a waitress."

"You are today," he replied.

"Ewan, what the hell are you talking about?"

He stood up and put his hands on his hips. "It's today's lesson."

"Waitressing?"

"No. Attitude adjustment."

She narrowed her eyes. "And just whose attitude are we adjusting?"

"Nat. You were complaining that you didn't have anyone to celebrate special events with. You keep making those silly comments about being a bitch and not having a lot of friends."

"Well, maybe I like being a bitch. I sort of think it's my one true talent."

He ruffled her hair. "I think sometimes you worry about the way people perceive you more than you care to admit. I thought maybe today you could learn how to practice restraint. Besides, it's Keira's day off and we're always busting our asses during the lunch shift."

She ignored that he needed her help, changing the subject back to the one that was bothering her most of all. "You think I need to learn restraint?" She sat up, trying to figure out why the idea of Ewan trying to change her personality hurt so badly. She *had* sort of signed up for this.

Ewan held up his finger to ward off the pain he must have seen building on her face. "Don't say a word. Just hear me out. Personally, I fucking love your personality. I think you're funny as shit and that caustic wit of yours is top-notch. You don't offend me, you don't scare me and, truth be told, listening to you eviscerate someone is probably on my list of top five turn-ons. However, you seemed to be concerned that you push people away with your comments and I thought this might be a good way for you to practice thinking before you speak. I thought this was what you wanted."

She took a deep breath and tried to formulate a coherent thought. "I sort of stopped listening at *I fucking love your personality*," she finally said. "No one's ever said those words to me."

Ewan laughed. "Hard to believe, eh?"

"Impossible." She grinned ruefully, wondering how he always managed to make her insides go to mush. She wasn't a wishy-washy little girl. She was a woman who knew better than to have her head turned by a few well-phrased words. Thing was, Ewan really looked as if he meant what he was saying. "Okay. This sounds like it could be a cool experiment."

Ewan stared at her for a moment. "Well, yeah, about that. While it's an experiment, I'd like to stress that the restaurant is my business and it only succeeds if my customers are happy and want to come back. I'd sort of consider it a personal favor if you—"

"Wouldn't speak my mind? Fuck up? Intimidate the patrons until they run screaming from the building?" she finished for him.

"All of those work for me."

"I'll behave." She rose from the bed and picked up the forest green shirt he'd brought for her. "We're gonna have to talk about your waitress uniforms, though." She wrinkled her nose at the shirt. "These are guy shirts."

"I suppose you think I should steal the Hooters idea and put my waitresses in too-tight tank tops? This is a family business, Nat. Plus, I don't think our regular waitress, Joyce, would go for it. She's pushing fifty and complains about her sagging breasts constantly."

Natalie shook her head. "You talk to your waitress about her tits?"

"She usually starts the subject. I just listen. I grew up with three very vocal sisters who complained about everything from period cramps and PMS to the under-wire in bras. I figure there's not much about the female body that can shock or embarrass me at this point."

She smiled. "In other words, you were raised right."

Ewan pulled her over to him with his hands on her waist. "I guess I was. How about a reward system for today's experiment? You seemed to like that last night."

"You know, I'm starting to suspect these so-called rewards are just your way of trying to get into my pants."

Ewan laughed. "Is it working?"

She pressed her finger to her lip and pretended to consider his question. "Maybe."

He kissed her quickly. "Get ready. I'll meet you down in the restaurant. Give you a brief orientation before we open."

TWO HOURS LATER, Natalie had decided Ewan could take his rewards and shove them up his tight, muscular, gorgeous ass.

She'd cleaned up two major drink spills, both done by the same little unruly brat whose mother couldn't control him if he was in a cage. She'd listened to a woman complain for ten minutes about Natalie screwing up her order—which she hadn't. Fucking bitch couldn't even remember what she'd asked for. One man snapped over her forgetting to bring his bread, even though any yahoo could see it was lunch hour, the restaurant was packed and she was running around like a chicken with her head cut off.

Jesus, people were rude. She'd nearly bitten her tongue off several times and it didn't look as though things were going to get much better as the afternoon progressed.

"Excuse me, miss." Natalie fought against rolling her eyes as the elderly woman at the corner table called her over…again.

"Yes, ma'am. What can I get for you *now*?" So far, the lady had beckoned her over for a slice of lemon in her water, more butter for her bread, an extra knife because she dropped hers and more napkins—each time starting some inane, longwinded conversation about the weather or her sister's cataract surgery.

"I was wondering about the dessert menu. Do you have one of those?"

"The desserts are listed on the regular menu." Which she'd taken back after getting the woman's lunch order. "I'll just run and get you one."

"Thank you, dear. You're new here, aren't you?"

Natalie nodded, trying to get away before the woman could ask any more questions. She wasn't so lucky.

"Are you from Baltimore?"

Natalie shook her head. "No, I live in Palm Springs.

I'm a friend of the Collins family and just helping out with the lunch rush today. I'm actually a photographer."

The woman seemed delighted by this new information. "A photographer! Oh, what a wonderful job. Are you one of those *National Geographic* photographers who travel all over the world taking pictures of nature and naked tribal women?"

Natalie laughed at the woman's question, though she could see it was a serious one. "I wish. I just run a regular old studio. Wedding photos and stuff like that."

"Nat, you've got an order up." Ewan passed her with a large tray of food. "Riley wanted me to let you know."

"I'll be right back with your dessert menu," she said to the customer.

The older woman waved at her and smiled. "Take your time."

She passed Ewan, admiring his muscular arms as he wielded the tray loaded with food with ease. She wondered how he could do this job day in and day out. As she grabbed the dessert menu, she watched him place the food in front of the customers—all of whom he seemed to know by name. He made a couple jokes as he gave them their food. It was clear he was a natural with people, but more than that, he really enjoyed talking to them, getting to know them. He'd stopped at every table since the restaurant opened— regardless of how of busy they were—and spoken a few words to each customer. Whether they were regulars or tourists, he found a way to make them all feel welcome.

Then she considered the way he'd treated her since day one. Friendly, open, kind. In Ewan's world, there were no strangers, just friends waiting to be made.

"Nat?" Ewan walked up next to her and she realized he'd caught her lollygagging. "You okay? Need a break?"

She shook her head. "No, I'm fine. You're really good at this."

"At what?"

"Running this restaurant. Being nice to people."

He laughed. "Being nice isn't exactly a hard thing, babydoll."

"Maybe not for you. I've been this close," she held up her thumb and forefinger, "to crushing some of these idiots with my bare hands."

"Well, we've got about an hour before it tapers off for the afternoon. What do you say we meet in my office at two? You can decompress to me all you want."

"I'm warning you now. You're gonna get an earful."

He gave her a peck on the cheek. "I'm really proud of you, Nat. You may not want to know this, but you're actually sort of a natural at waitressing."

"Bite. Your. Tongue." With that, she walked away before he could see the secret grin his compliment had provoked.

AN HOUR LATER, Ewan gestured to her with a quick jerk of his head and she followed him into this office. It was down a small hallway from the main dining room and across from the kitchen. She could hear the muffled clanging of dishes through the walls even after Ewan shut the door. She turned to face him and fought down the sudden dampness lining her panties as she watched him lock the door.

"Hit me with your best shot," he said as he crossed the room toward her. He didn't stop until he had her backed up against his desk.

"That loud-mouth woman with the little brat needs classes in parenting."

"Agreed." Then he startled her with a long, deep kiss.

She wrapped her arms around his neck, falling easily into his warm embrace. How did he manage to capture her interest with affection? She wasn't a kisser, a hugger, a cuddler. She'd never craved these things before Ewan. Now she wanted them more than a cold beer on a hot summer day.

He broke off the kiss, lightly rubbing his nose against hers. "Anything else?"

"That obnoxious asshole who bitched about the lack of bread should have been thanking me. More bread was the last thing he needed."

"Agreed." Ewan repeated the line and the kiss and she decided she liked the way he held a bitch session.

When he pulled away, she realized she was struggling to think of any more complaints. The anger that had been building in her chest most of the day was quickly diminishing.

"I didn't mess up that stupid woman's order. She asked for the special. I swear she did."

"I heard her. She *did* ask for the special."

Natalie frowned, confused. "But you told me to take the food back…to get her the hamburger."

"It wasn't worth fighting about. Besides, Mrs. Davis is a regular in here. She mentioned once that she cares for her mother who suffers from Alzheimer's. Sometimes she's just tired and grumpy."

"Damn," Natalie muttered. "Now I feel like shit."

Ewan laughed. "I'm not trying to make you feel bad, Nat. You couldn't have known that. I'm just trying to show you that sometimes you don't always know what's going on in another person's life. That haggard mom is going through a nasty divorce. She's way too slack with her kid, probably because she feels guilty for her failing marriage."

She closed her eyes. "See, I *am* a bitch."

He cupped her cheeks with his palms, pulling her face closer to his. "Open your eyes. Look at me."

She obeyed, surprised to see his face so close to hers.

"You are not a bitch. You're way too hard on yourself. You set these high expectations for yourself and I think you just hold other people to the same standards. There's nothing wrong with that."

"So what's the sob story on the bread guy?"

"Oh, he *is* just an asshole. You had him pegged right in the first minute."

She laughed. "Well, thank the Lord. I'm one for twenty. That older woman, the one who sat in the corner table?"

Ewan acknowledged he knew who she was talking about with a nod.

"She was kinda cool. What's up with her?"

"Mrs. Duvall. Her husband passed away a couple of years ago and I think she's lonely. She comes in here twice a week for lunch and she always manages to find a way to call us all over to chat. I usually join her for a bit, but she seemed to prefer your company today."

Once she'd returned with the woman's dessert, she'd been drawn into a conversation that she'd genuinely enjoyed.

When she thought about it, she'd had more fun these past three days than she'd had in years and she suddenly wasn't looking forward to returning to Palms Springs. What if she went home and the heavy feelings came back? She wasn't sure she wanted to go back to her monotonous days, her quiet apartment.

She tried to shut down her thoughts of leaving on Saturday. The unwelcome notion of leaving Ewan had jarred her more than once over the past few days. Now, like then, she put the nonsense away. He was an acquaintance, Teagan's brother. Nothing more. She couldn't let him be anything more.

For now, she wanted to revel in the newfound lightness. Here in Baltimore she'd managed to find a place where she could relax, put away her worries, her gloominess, her sleepless nights, even if only for a week. She'd use this time to pick up the pieces and come Saturday, she would go home. She'd be strong again. Ready to roll with the punches.

"And now," Ewan said, grasping her hand and

tugging her behind the desk with him. "Maybe we could revisit that 'making out as a form of relaxation' lesson from last night. I mean, you've had a rough afternoon." He lifted her shirt over her head, pulling it off before she had a moment to realize his intent.

"Hey. You know, just talking it out…I feel much better now."

He frowned. "You do. You sure? I don't mind going the extra mile if you're still a little tense."

She laughed but didn't try to put her shirt back on. "You're incorrigible."

"I'm horny, Nat. Throw a dog a bone."

"Look's like this dog already has one." She ran her hand along the front placket of his pants and he groaned.

"Is that a yes?"

She considered his question for a moment. "We're just playing right? I mean—"

He placed a finger on her lips. "We're two adults sharing an attraction. It's chemistry, remember?"

She'd never experienced more than quick fucks with men she never cared if she saw again. She wasn't loose by any stretch of the imagination and it had been too fucking long since she'd indulged. When the need got to be too much and her vibrator stopped cutting it, she simply found someone to ease the pain. Something told her Ewan wouldn't be an easy lover, nor would he be easily dismissed. Casual sex she could handle. Unfortunately, nothing she did with Ewan ever felt casual. "Just second base, maybe third. No homers."

"I'll take third," he said with a grin.

"I said *maybe* third. What if someone comes in?" she asked, her question in conflict with her actions as she helped Ewan strip away her bra as well.

"The door's locked, remember?" Ewan bent down and took one of her nipples roughly into his mouth, no foreplay, no preamble, just straightforward, glorious sucking.

"Oh my God, you're good at that." She gripped his head, tangling her fingers in his hair to hold him in place. He continued his torment after she moved up onto the desk. She captured his hips with her legs, pulling his erection toward her. Even through multiple layers of clothing she could feel his hard length. She rubbed against him and he moaned.

"Dammit, Nat. Second won't be enough."

He unhooked her pants, lifting her ass off the desk with one hand while tugging her pants and panties over her hips and down her legs. "Kick off your shoes. I want to see you totally naked."

She complied, but couldn't resist looking over her shoulder toward the door once more. She was completely undressed while Ewan had yet to remove a single stitch of clothing. To make matters worse, they were in a somewhat public place.

"No one will come in, babydoll. I promise."

"Aren't you going to take your clothes off?"

He shook his head. "Not if you're serious about third."

.  .  .

NATALIE APPEARED to want to say more, but her words turned into a sigh when his fingers lightly brushed her clit. She spread her legs farther and he accepted her invitation, running his hand along her slit, cupping her mound in his palm. Her breathing turned to panting and he knew she was struggling to remain quiet.

He pressed two fingers into her wet heat and she groaned softly. "How long has it been, Nat? How long since you had a living, breathing man touch this sweet pussy? Your fucking vibrator doesn't count."

She closed her eyes but he refused to let her retreat. Once his fingers were lodged to the hilt, he froze. "Open your eyes. Open them and answer my question."

"I don't know," she whispered. "Maybe a year or so."

A year. She'd been alone for a year. No wonder she'd been wound up tighter than a spring when she'd shown up here. Of course, given the way just touching her hot pussy was sending every ounce of blood in his body straight to his groin, it was safe to say it had been too long for him too.

"What about you?" she asked, her question ending with a tiny squeak as he pressed deeper.

"Nine months, three days, forty-seven minutes and —" He glanced toward the clock on the wall, but Natalie's laughter ended the joke.

"I think I got the message. Too long," she said.

He silenced her with a brief kiss while shoving his fingers inside her. He thought perhaps he should slow his pace, gentle his thrusts, but her moans drove him on. She moved toward his fingers, begging with every softly muttered "more."

He finger-fucked her harder than he'd ever dared to take a woman and still she begged for more. His head swam as the truth of the moment played out for him. He'd jokingly blamed chemistry for their attraction, but now he wondered if he hadn't been right in his estimation. She was made for him. Some small certainty had expressed that opinion the first time they'd met—the voice within growing louder and more insistent with each meeting. Now it was screaming inside his head and he wouldn't—no, he couldn't—ignore it anymore.

"Come for me, Nat." He whispered his command and her body responded instantly in an explosion he was certain she felt to her toes.

"Ah, ah, oh God," she whispered. He knew she wanted to scream, could see it in the stiffness of her body, the tension in her face, but she was aware of the hustle and bustle of the restaurant just outside the door.

It didn't matter what sounds she made. She was beautiful when she came.

"Seven days isn't gonna be long enough. Lie back, close your eyes. I wanna see you come again."

"Again?" she asked.

Ewan chuckled. "Oh, hell yeah. I wonder if you taste as sweet as you look."

"Oh look, what do you know? The third-base coach really *is* waving you in," she teased.

He laughed at her invitation and attacked her clit,

sucking the swollen nub the same way he'd taken her nipples. He devoured her like a starving man.

She bit her lip to try to hold back her cries and he chuckled.

"I can't wait to hear all those noises you're bottling up."

She moaned. "I'm not usually a quiet lover."

He looked up at her. "You just spent the whole morning practicing restraint. Consider this another part of the same lesson."

"This isn't restraint. It's torture."

He bent back down, his tongue plunging into her depths, and she squealed at the unexpected movement.

"Masochist," she said through gritted teeth.

His mouth drifted lower, rimming the outer edges of her anus.

"Hey," she protested breathlessly.

"I'm warning you now, babydoll, there's no part of you I won't touch, won't take."

She shuddered at his darkly erotic threat.

"That's a little farther than third."

He chuckled. "I'm working up to a grand slam. When I take you the first time, it's gonna be in a bed somewhere private and we're going to have hours to do it right. And you are definitely going to scream your head off."

Ewan pushed two fingers inside her pussy while sucking on her clit.

"Dammit," she cried.

"No smartass reply?"

"I'm sort of struggling to remember my name right now. Less talk, more action."

He laughed as he felt the beginning of her second climax build, her inner muscles clenching his fingers tightly.

"Ewan!" His name came out with a gasp and he doubled his efforts, his fingers moving faster, deeper.

"Come on, babydoll," he murmured, his lips brushing her mons as he spoke. "Come on my fingers. Let me feel how much you want me."

His words triggered an immediate response and she shuddered with the effort of remaining quiet.

"Fuck," she muttered, shaking as Ewan continued to pump his fingers inside her. He stood up, caging her body against the hard surface.

"Is that the best you can do?" His fingers never stilled, never stopped thrusting. His challenging question worked as he felt her body accept the dare.

"Dammit, Ewan. I can't do it again."

"Yes, you can," he commanded. His lips claimed hers as he fed her the sharp taste of her juices from his lips. She licked at him hungrily as he added a third finger to the first two, his thumb rubbing her clit mercilessly as she bucked beneath him. He'd never pushed a woman like this, never wanted her pleasure more than his own. Seeing her tremble under his touch, hearing her muffled cries, he felt as if he'd spent his whole life merely waiting for this one moment. It was too much, too fucking fantastically much.

When he removed the third finger from her pussy, he upped the ante by inviting his pinky to the party, shoving it roughly into her ass. She jerked, lost control. She gripped the back of his neck, pulling his face toward hers. She plunged her tongue into his mouth and he knew she was riding on pure, animalistic instinct.

He captured her scream as she came yet again, silencing her moans with his tongue as her pussy clenched greedily at his fingers, crushing them, covering them with her hot come.

"God, baby," he whispered as she trembled. "You're so fucking hot, Nat. I'm never going to get enough of you, of those orgasms. I thought you were going to break my fingers." He rested his forehead against hers as they gasped, sharing the same air. "I can't wait to get my cock inside you."

"Do it now."

He groaned, her words firing his body like a machine gun. He could take her now, but he knew her body was making the request, not her head. "Not here, Nat. Please, not here."

The words were dragged from his throat and he was relieved when she didn't press him. Her sudden silence proved her head was already catching up, already regretting the request.

He glanced at the clock and slowly pushed himself off her body. She glanced down, saw the distinct outline of his erection through his pants.

"Ewan," she pointed at his cock, "let me—"

"No. God no. I pull my cock out and there's no way this thing ends the way you want. I was an ass to start this in the office. I don't know what to say. You make me lose my head."

She smiled sadly. "The feeling's mutual."

He took a deep breath, fought to lighten the mood. "Besides, I walk around in this condition pretty much nonstop every time you're in the state of Maryland. It's nothing a cold shower and hand job won't take care of. I have about an hour until the dinner rush starts, so I'm going to run upstairs."

He grasped her shirt and tugged it over her head. The sooner she was covered up, the easier this would be.

"Um, aren't you forgetting something?" she asked when he bent down to pick up her pants.

He reached out, tweaking her nipple through the shirt. "I like how you look with no bra on."

"I'm not walking around like this. This chemical reaction you keep talking about seems to work both ways. You walk around with a hard-on. I walk around with—" She pointed at her nipples, poking through her shirt. "I'm bound to take an eye out."

He laughed but ignored her comment, helping her put her pants back on as she blushed. He loved seeing her cheeks flush. He was so used to her cynicism, her lack of embarrassment. Seeing her overwhelmed and horny was sexy as hell.

"Do you need help with the dinner shift?" she asked. "I mean, I could help if you wanted. Probably wouldn't hurt for me to, um, practice that being nice thing a little more."

"I'd love some help, but Nat, don't get *too* good at

biting your tongue. I'd prefer it if you didn't hold anything back with me."

He'd meant what he'd said this morning. He liked her exactly as she was.

"Oh, you don't need to worry about that, hotshot. If you annoy me or piss me off, you're gonna know it."

"That's my girl," he said, kissing her quickly. "I'm going to run upstairs and get that shower."

"I'm going to stay here and put my bra back on."

He shook his head dejectedly. "Spoilsport." He wiggled his eyebrows, closing the office door behind him as he left.

He rested against the other side of the door and tried to take a deep breath. He was getting tired of cold showers. He needed a game plan. His eyes landed on a bulletin board hanging on the wall across from him. Local businesses could put up their flyers, business cards. Patrons waiting to use the restrooms usually bided the time reading the information.

Ewan spotted a flyer for one of the local five-star hotels. It was located on the Inner Harbor, was super swanky with a gourmet restaurant on the first floor. He pulled the flyer down from the board and grinned.

He'd just figured out his next lesson—and Miss Natalie Miller wasn't going to know what hit her.

# CHAPTER FIVE

Tuesday…

Natalie was awake when Ewan came into her room early Tuesday morning. She was sitting on the bed waiting for him, and he didn't let her down.

"You're up." He was clearly surprised to see her awake and dressed as he walked into her room. She thought he also looked a wee bit disappointed.

"Yep. Getting an early start today. I have plans."

"You do?" he asked.

"Teagan, Riley and Keira are going shopping for a wedding dress and they've invited me to tag along."

"Ah. That's brave of you. Or maybe stupid would be more accurate."

She laughed at his horrified expression. She didn't want to admit she was leaning toward the stupidity angle herself, and that guilt was driving her to spend an entire day with the Collins sisters. She'd been in Baltimore for four days and she'd yet to take any of the pictures she'd promised she'd get for Sky's video.

"Very funny. You know, it would serve you right if I told your sisters what you just said."

He actually appeared to go pale. "You wouldn't dare."

She laughed. "Chicken shit. What do you want? Why are you always invading my personal space?"

Ewan plopped down on the bed beside her and bent close. "I thought you liked having me *in* your personal space."

The way he stressed the word *in* sent an immediate surge of arousal to her pussy and she marveled at how he could turn her on with just a few words. Usually it took a good deal of effort, or lube, to get her wet and ready.

"Why are you here, Ewan?" She tried to sound annoyed, but she was afraid her breathless tone sounded more like a plea.

"Do you have plans for dinner?" he asked.

She shook her head.

"Well, you do now. I'm going to take you somewhere fancy, so dress up."

She tried not to be disappointed when he rose without even trying to steal a kiss.

"Have fun with my sisters. I've made reservations for seven."

"Reservations? Wow. Guess McDonald's is out."

He smiled. "It's not McDonald's. And Nat, wear your hair down. I love it when you leave it loose."

He gave her a quick wave goodbye as he left her alone again. He'd made reservations? She lay across her bed and smiled. He'd made reservations and he liked her hair loose. She reveled in that knowledge for a few minutes before kicking herself for acting like a giddy school girl.

*Jeez, Nat. Get a grip. It's just a date.*

A date. With Ewan.

Shit.

---

NATALIE FINISHED her dessert and tried to remember when she'd had a nicer evening. She'd been surprised when Ewan brought her to one of the most opulent hotels in Baltimore. She'd heard of the restaurant from Sky and she knew it was one of the city's finest.

Ewan took a sip of his wine and gave her a wolfish look. She leaned back and gave in to the blissful feeling she'd tried to suppress all night. She was out on a date with Ewan Collins and she was having a wonderful time. If someone would have told her a week ago she'd be here, she'd have laughed them out of town.

In the past, it had been easy to hold Ewan at a distance, pretend her feelings didn't extend beyond the bonds of an occasional friendship. She wasn't really sure what had changed. Maybe he'd weakened her resistance. Maybe she'd been an easy mark, given her gloominess. Either way, she couldn't find it within herself to give a shit. She was having fun, she was sleeping, and she was going to have sex with the hottest guy on the planet. Yesterday in his office had only whetted her desire for more. At this point, she'd decided the consequences could be damned. She wanted him and he wanted her.

"Jesus, Nat. You keep looking at me like that and I'm likely to throw you over this table, hike up that skirt and take you right now, regardless of who's around."

She laughed. "I think at this point, you wouldn't hear any arguments." She moved closer. "I wanna crawl under this table, take your cock in my mouth and suck you dry."

Ewan choked on his wine, her words taking him unaware, and she grinned.

"I've booked a room." He said the words hesitantly and it took her a moment to make sense of them.

"A room?"

"In the hotel."

She paused to consider his proposition. She wanted him more than she'd ever wanted any man. But the idea that's he'd planned this whole evening, wined and dined her with the intention of seducing her, left her suddenly uncertain.

"Fuck. Nat, I'm sorry. It was presumptuous. I know."

She quickly shook her head. "No, Ewan. We've been steadily marching in this direction for three years. I…you just surprised me. That's all."

"Are you attracted to me?" he asked.

"You know I am. Christ, haven't I proven I am? Yes."

"Natalie. We can go home or we can go upstairs. The decision is completely yours."

She looked at his serious, beloved face and smiled. "How could you think for a minute I'd say no to you? I want to go upstairs, Ewan. I want it so badly."

His smile was genuine, beautiful. "Come on. I don't think I'm going to be able to wait much longer to hold you. You are so gorgeous tonight."

"Sweet talker." He paid the bill and she tried to ignore the growing heat in her body. She was going to sleep with Ewan tonight. She'd had sex before. Scratched the itch, so to speak. She couldn't remember ever waiting for sex with more anticipation.

As the elevator took them up to their room, Ewan kissed her gently and she felt like a princess, the most cherished woman on the planet.

He held her hand as they walked along the lushly carpeted hallway. "So you were awfully sure of yourself," she said as they paused outside the door.

"I don't know if it was confidence as much as hope. I want you, Natalie. I've wanted you for years." She'd intended her comment as a joke, a smartass way to bring a bit a levity to a moment that was suddenly too serious, too important.

Ewan's response threw everything into another realm and she realized whether she admitted it or not, tonight was different. Tonight was special.

He slid the card key through the slot and gently pressed on her back, guiding her inside. She gasped when she saw the room. It was lit by several candles and the king-sized bed was covered with luscious, bright-red rose petals. The Jacuzzi tub at the side of the room was filled, steam rising from the hot water, and there was a bottle of champagne chilling on the counter of the wet bar.

"This looks like…" She couldn't make herself say the word.

He smiled. "The honeymoon suite. It is. It's a Tuesday night. It wasn't booked, so I grabbed it. I remembered some of your comments about romance and your lack of belief, so I thought I'd bring you here. Prove to you that it really does exist."

"Tonight's lesson," she whispered. "It's romance?"

"It *does* exist, Nat. And if any woman ever deserved to be romanced, it's you."

She swallowed against the lump his words had provoked. He was wooing her, romancing her. Giving her the most precious moment of her life.

"Ewan," she said, but the rest of her words failed. Nothing she could say would tell him what this moment meant to her.

"Are you sure you want this, Nat? Sure you want *me*?"

"You know I do."

He gave her a crooked grin. "Then I'm yours. Come here."

She walked into his arms as if she were returning home after years away. There was no question in her mind that in this moment in time, she was exactly where she wanted to be.

He kissed her softly and when she tried to deepen the embrace, he pulled away with a sexy grin. He walked over to the table by the window and pressed play on a CD player she hadn't noticed. She gave him a quizzical look.

"I came over this afternoon to pick up the key, drop off a few things." He reached out for her hand as a slow song began to play. "Dance with me, Nat."

She bit her lips to stop the slight quiver his sensual gaze provoked. She took his hand, let him pull her close, let the music take over as they gently swayed and turned. She rested her head against his chest, felt the strong, steady beat beneath her cheek as he placed a soft kiss on the top of her head.

She'd never danced with anyone like this, though she'd photographed it, captured this moment a million times in the past. Always the observer, never the dancer. "I like this song. What is it?"

"*Falling Slowly*. It's from a movie I saw once."

"It's nice."

They didn't say anything else as the song continued, simply held each other and moved. As the music drifted away into another song, Ewan grasped her head in his hands, smiled as he bent down to steal the perfect kiss. His lips rubbed lightly against hers, enticing her to open her mouth. She sucked in a deep breath of his air, reaching out to taste him as well. Their tongues met, touched, played. If there was ever a moment in her life she'd want to freeze, this was it. She wanted to stop time, wrap up the occasion in tissue paper and tuck it in her pocket, so she could always pull it out and come right back here.

He kissed her cheek before turning her away from

him. He draped her hair over her shoulder so he could lower the zipper on her dress. Then he slid the silky cloth over her shoulders and she kicked it off when it hit her ankles.

"Oh damn," he whispered, and she didn't bother to hold back her wicked smile.

She looked at him over her shoulder. "Like what you see?"

His gaze was locked on her back. No, she thought, definitely lower, as he studied her garter, her stockings, the bare skin her thong didn't even begin to cover.

"You take my breath away, Nat."

His comment caused the same effect in her and she smiled as she turned to face him again. Her fingers tangled with his as they fought to unbutton his shirt. After everything they'd done the past few days, she'd yet to see him without his shirt. She couldn't wait to unwrap the present, discover what treasures lay beneath. He slid the shirt off, dropping it on top of her discarded dress.

She couldn't resist touching him and she ran her fingers along the defined muscles of his chest, around his nipples. Bending forward, she ran her tongue along his pec, grinning when his tiny nub tightened.

"I want to see the rest of you," she said, her hands drifting to relieve him of his belt. He helped her, pushing his pants and boxers off in one swoop, kicking them off along with his shoes. She swallowed heavily. She'd felt his hard length before, but the true sight of it was magnificent. He was beautiful, though she knew he wouldn't want to hear her use that word.

She imagined photographing him, capturing his defined lines, using shadows and lighting to accentuate every curve that made him uniquely masculine and sexy.

Ewan gripped the elastic waistband of her thong, pulling it over her hips and allowing it to fall. "It's just going to be in my way," he said and she laughed, delighted by his honesty, his ability to make the night magical and whimsical at the same time.

He kissed her again and, as one, they moved toward the bed. She tumbled down onto her back and Ewan crawled over her. He pressed against her knees, pushing her legs apart so he could kneel between them. She gasped when he ran his hands through the evidence of her arousal and she cried out when he used that wetness to slide two fingers inside her. He didn't stop once he'd breached her; rather, he worked his fingers against her flesh until she was writhing beneath him, begging for more.

Ewan continued to caress her with his hand. She twisted her head, struggling for air as he touched her deeply. She was assaulted by the scent of the roses as she moved, reminded again of how much he'd done to make this night perfect. He'd given her so much.

"I want you inside me," she said, reaching out, trying to draw him closer to her.

He grabbed a condom from the side table. "I meant to take this slow, Nat, but I need—"

"I don't want slow. I just want you. Please." Her last word fell out in a breathless sigh and he covered her, caging her below his large frame. He placed the head of his cock at the entrance to her body, stopping for only a second.

His eyes met hers. "I'm going to make love to you, Natalie. I don't want you to mistake this for anything else."

She only had time to nod once before he pushed into her, proving with his actions the truth of his words. He was showering her with love, with beauty, with peace and freedom. Those concepts would terrify her later, she had no doubts about that. But for tonight, she wanted them more than she'd ever wanted anything in her life.

Over and over, he came into her until she came twice, each climax unique. The first hit her fast, overpowering her senses as she screamed and she was only vaguely aware that Ewan was still moving. When the second came, it built slower, hung on longer, each of Ewan's thrusts sending spirals of pleasure coated with pain to every nerve ending in her body. It was simply too much, too good. She moaned, pleaded, begged for more. Ewan never stopped. He gave her everything.

"God, Nat," he cried as she felt the spark of her third orgasm. She thought briefly her life was passing before her eyes because surely this one would kill her. No one could withstand this much pleasure and live to tell about it. He groaned and she knew he was close. She thanked God he was close.

"Come with me," she said through gritted teeth. He groaned as he came, the pulsing throbs of his cock shoving her into another climax. Her entire body shook with the delight, her skin super sensitive and ultra aware of the sweat running down the side of her face, the tightness of the rose petals as they clung to her back, Ewan's labored breathing against her neck, the weight of his body as he collapsed on top of her.

He turned to lie beside her, pulling his cock out by millimeters since each slight movement sent her inner muscles into a fresh round of contractions, causing her to cry out, hold him close.

He cupped her face when it was apparent retreating from her body wasn't going to be easy. He kissed her and grinned. "Like a bandage," he whispered, as he quickly withdrew completely.

"Ah," she sighed, wincing as her body rejected his abandonment. She quivered in the aftermath, struggled to close her thighs. It had been too long. No, she thought, as she looked at Ewan and recalled his love-making. She'd never been with someone like that...and she suddenly felt as shy and uncertain as a virgin. "Well, that was interesting," she said, forcing her voice to return to its natural state.

He shook his head, pulling her closer and kissing her face, her eyes, her brow. "Don't," he said, his voice husky, almost hoarse. "Don't go there. Not yet."

She laid her head on his chest and closed her eyes against the tears gathering there. How did he know? How did he always know?

She swallowed against the lump in her throat and decided she owed him something real, something true.

"I've never experienced anything like that, Ewan. Anything so..." Her insecurities, her pride kept her from speaking the word.

It didn't matter. Ewan knew. "Perfect."

That was definitely the word that had been hovering on the edge of her lips and she fell silent, unable to refute the truth, though terrified to admit it. He ran his fingers through her hair and she melted further in his arms. She'd never wanted this affection, this closeness in the past, but she could no more leave his arms now than she could cut off her own nose. She needed to be here.

When the silence became too heavy, she looked up, consumed with curiosity. What was he thinking? Was he as floored as her?

The questions clogged her throat. One week was all he'd asked for. One week to play their game. It was all he owed her and all she wanted. It was time to get back on track. She dug deep to find the Natalie she could control, the one she could understand, but she'd deserted her, left her high and dry.

"So," she began, cursing the shyness in her voice. "Do you think we can we do it again?"

He laughed at her request. "Oh hell yeah, but later. For now, I gotta rest up. I may be young, babydoll, but I'm not Superman."

She laughed, relieved he so quickly reverted to form. The fun, laidback Ewan she could handle. It was the passionate lover, the romantic man who was wreaking havoc on her head and…

She closed her eyes, afraid to think the word. It came anyway.

*Heart.*

He was touching her heart—and it scared the hell out of her.

---

EWAN ROUSED SEVERAL HOURS LATER. A quick glance at the clock confirmed it was a couple hours before dawn. Natalie was wrapped up in his arms, her head using his chest as a pillow. Her breath was warm, soft against his skin, and he closed his eyes, savoring the feeling.

She was magnificent. Amazing. Everything he'd dreamed she'd be, but so much more. He'd always suspected her sensual side, knew from her fiery nature outside the bedroom she'd be incredible between the sheets. All he'd needed to do was convince her to leave her hang-ups at the door. So far, so good, but he didn't harbor any illusions he'd made it safely to shore yet. There was still a lot of fight left in his woman. He just hoped his stamina outlasted hers.

He gently lifted her head, placing it on the pillow. She murmured but didn't wake, instead moving to her back. He wrapped the blanket around her as he rose from the bed and went into the bathroom. He chuckled as he looked at himself in the mirror. He had at least a dozen rose petals stuck to his body. He peeled them off before brushing his teeth.

Ewan studied his reflection, trying to ignore what he knew was running through his mind. He'd been enamored of Natalie Miller since they'd first met. Like any young guy, he'd dreamed of capturing her for a night or two, plotted ways to get her into his bed—inviting her to Baltimore for art shows, festivals, concerts. The more she rebuffed his advances, the harder he tried. Soon, however, he was devising ways to get her to come to Baltimore simply because he wanted to see her. His advances became less about sex and more about her. She fascinated him, enticed him.

He scowled. He was in way over his head. He was in love with Nat and he knew it was going to take a hell of a lot longer than a week to claim her closed-up heart. Something was holding her back, keeping her from making the leap from a solitary life to one shared with family, friends, a lover. He suspected she was protecting a secret, something so painful she felt the need to shut the world out, keep everyone she knew at arm's length. Until she trusted him enough to confide in him, he wasn't sure anything he did or said would bridge that gap.

They needed more time. Sighing heavily, he shook off his heavy thoughts. It was only Wednesday and they were still on Tuesday's lesson. Three days. He had three days to convince Natalie to trust him, to show her that having an exciting life wasn't worth a damn if you didn't have someone to share it with.

Tiptoeing back into the bedroom, he spotted her camera on the nightstand. He'd been carrying it around since taking it from her on the fishing boat. He kept waiting for her to ask for it back, but she hadn't yet. He knew she had other, bigger cameras with her. The little pocket-sized job he'd taken must be her personal one, while she used the professional cameras for her more serious shots.

She looked so beautiful, her blonde hair across the pillow, her usually tense, alert features soft, peaceful. He picked up the camera and snapped a quick shot. He thought the flash would disturb her but he must have worn her out more than he realized.

Grinning, he slowly dragged the sheets away from her body, watching as, bit by bit, more of her luscious body was revealed. He stopped after baring her breasts, his gaze studying her pink nipples as they went tight with the cool air. He continued moving the sheet down, stopping again to study her mons. She kept her light hair trimmed close and he felt the urge to run his fingers through it. Removing the sheet entirely, he climbed back on the bed, carefully spreading her legs so he could kneel between them.

She sighed, but again, she didn't stir.

"Rise and shine, Sleeping Beauty," he whispered as he leaned forward and dragged his tongue against her slit. A tiny bit of moisture met his lips and he glanced up, not surprised to find her sleepy gaze on him.

"Hungry?" she asked, and he chuckled at her mocking wit. She used sarcasm as a shield. He'd realized that from their first meeting. Knowing that made it easier to dismiss, and he knew she was confused by his lack of offense each time she made some cutting comment, provoking no response.

"Starving," he replied. He lightly ran his tongue along her drenched flesh, thrilled by the copious amount of juice her body had produced. Regardless of her confusion about her feelings, her body was opening to him, inviting him in. He pushed his tongue into her sheath as her hands found his hair. She caressed his face, his cheeks, as he savored and sampled every part of her. When her response to his intimate kisses turned from comfort to desire, he moved over her, stopping only to place hot, deep kisses on each nipple.

"Need you," she whispered.

He continued upward until his lips found hers and they kissed for hours, days, until the heat between their bodies threatened to consume them.

"Please," she cried at last, pulling her face away from him. "Please, Ewan."

He reached for a condom but she stopped him. "Do you have to wear that?"

"You tell me."

"I'm on birth control. I'm clean."

"So am I," he replied.

"Then don't wear it. I don't want you to—"

He kissed her when she stumbled over her request. He didn't need to hear the words. The idea that she wanted this kind of intimacy, this level of trust, gave him hope. For the first time since the week began, he thought perhaps he was making progress.

He placed his cock at her entrance and pushed forward with care. Once he was lodged to the hilt, he remained there, relishing the warm solace of simply being held within her body. He kissed her again and they began a gentle, smooth rocking. Their connection felt more important this time and they stayed linked together, touching, kissing, tasting. He held her gaze with his and watched her implode quietly, allowing her orgasm to pull his climax along as well. He felt each pulse of his cock filling her with his come. He was marking her in the most personal way he knew.

This was it, he thought. She was destined to be his true love or his ultimate heartbreak.

He rolled them to their sides, careful not to disengage, not to leave her body. He wasn't willing to give this feeling up. The Jacuzzi caught his eye. "How would you feel about a nice long soak?"

"Mmm, that sounds like a great idea. Can we drink the champagne too?"

"It's four o'clock in the morning."

"I don't care," she admitted.

"Neither do I."

After popping the cork on the bottle, he checked the water temperature and started the jets as she poured them each a glass of the bubbly wine.

As they sank into the water, Natalie sighed and grinned. "This is heaven on earth."

He agreed with a lazy nod. His body was aching in muscles he didn't know he had. "Tonight was great, Nat."

She smiled. "Is this the part of the evening where I impress my teacher with all my newfound intelligence about life and score some rewards?"

He tried to ignore the annoyance that accompanied her question. He didn't want tonight to be about learning a lesson. Rather than reveal his feelings, he forced a grin. "Haven't you had enough rewards?"

"Never." Her answer reached him on a whisper and

he silently prayed that answer was true. He bent closer and kissed her.

"So what did you learn?"

"I think you were trying to show me that it's okay to let go every once in while. That there's nothing wrong with letting yourself have something you want."

"And you wanted *me*?"

"I told you I thought you were hot."

Her comment rubbed against the grain as he felt her trying to put this whole evening in the sex category, rather than the lovemaking one. He tried to ignore her words. Sarcasm was Natalie's way. He knew better than to let her get under his skin.

"What about the romance? The soft music? The candles? The rose petals?" He felt like a jerk for returning her volley with his own cynicism. She blinked twice at his tone and he knew he was being a shithead, lashing out.

"That was all nice." Her response was quiet, uncertain.

"I'm just kidding, Nat. You learned exactly what I hoped you would."

"No, I don't think I did. I suck at romance. Suck at all that sweet shit. My sister, on the other hand, would have eaten tonight up with a spoon."

He remained quiet, hopeful. She'd just cracked a door and he knew it. She'd never volunteered information about her sister, though he knew the woman must have been a huge part of Natalie's life.

"Yvonne loved romantic movies, devoured romance novels—reading at least three a week. I used to tell her she was wasting her time on that garbage. That romance was the ultimate female fantasy and as likely to occur in real life as aliens coming to live amongst us."

"Haven't you ever seen *Men in Black*? The aliens are already here."

She laughed at his joke, but continued talking. "She used to date all the time. She was gorgeous, vivacious, friendly and fun. Everything I wasn't."

"That's not true, Nat. You're too hard on yourself."

"I'm not saying I'm a terrible person, Ewan. Really, I'm not. I know I'm smart. I'm cocky enough to think I'm very good at my job. This isn't a self-esteem issue. I've just always found it difficult to fit in, to forge relationships."

"That whole *people annoy me* thing?"

She smiled ruefully. "Maybe my problem is I think too highly of myself. I'm very intolerant, aren't I?"

He shook his head. "I don't think so. Besides, you do fine hanging out with me, my family, Sky."

She paused at that and looked at him. "You all seem to be the exceptions, rather than the norm. And in your case, I suspect it's because you have a bit of a sadomasochistic streak in you."

"What?" he asked.

"You must be in to pain to put up with all the abuse I pile on your head," she replied with a grin.

"Never thought of that. You may be right." They laughed together and the conversation died for a moment.

"How old was Yvonne when she died?" He hated to bring the playful mood down, but he'd never move ahead with Natalie if they didn't leap this hurdle. It was becoming clear Yvonne's death had played a big role in why Natalie didn't open herself up to close relationships.

"Twenty-three. I was twenty-four. We were born only ten months apart."

"Oh damn. You realize the not-so-nice term for that is Irish twins?"

She grinned. "Yeah, I've heard that expression before. How about that? I'm Irish too."

Natalie closed her eyes, rested her head against tub. He didn't like the distance so he shifted them, moved her until she sat between his legs, her back laying against his chest and her head on his shoulder. He suspected this conversation may be easier if it wasn't done face-to-face.

"You said it was a car accident?"

Natalie nodded. "She'd gone out one night to a party. She wasn't drinking. It wasn't anything like that. Yvonne rarely drank. It was just late and the police think she fell asleep at the wheel. She ran off the road and hit a tree."

"That must've been hard for you."

"I was supposed to go to the party with her."

"What?" Ewan could hear the pain lacing every word and his heart broke for her. Suddenly he understood.

"I bailed at the last minute. I hate parties, social situations, always have. I lied to her. Said I had a headache. If I'd been in that car with her, she wouldn't have—"

"Natalie, no. Life is one big *what if*. It's not your fault your sister died."

"Oh yeah," she said, her tone alerting him that cynical Nat was about to reemerge. "I've spent thousands of dollars in therapy for that answer. Must be true, right? I mean, *all* those psychiatrists can't be wrong."

"It wasn't your fault." He wished there was something he could say to make her believe him, but he was fighting a decade's worth of guilt and recrimination. He grasped her shoulders, turned her until she faced him. "It wasn't your fault."

"I don't want to talk about this anymore."

"Then when, Nat? When are you going to talk about it? When are you going to let this go and move on?"

"I'm moving on. I've been living and breathing and moving on for ten fucking years, Ewan. Ten years."

He didn't know what to say. What words he could offer that would comfort her, take away the agony he saw in her face, erase the erroneous belief that she was to blame.

"You're right. You've moved on." Rather than say more, he went with his gut, went with the instinct that said he knew what she needed more than words. He kissed her.

She fell into his embrace, clung to him like a child seeking solace during a storm. He felt her hands trembling as she reached up and wrapped them around his neck. She dove into the deep end and he pulled her out farther, gave her this moment, this time to wipe out the pain, to help her put the past away even if it was only for a little while.

He knew she never put it away for long.

Their kisses exploded like lightning flashing in the air around them as their tongues, their teeth fought a tug of war, a battle of give and take. She nipped his lower lip and he tasted the tangy, metallic flavor of his own blood. He reached up, gripped her hair, tugged at it in his attempts to hold her captive to his lips, his body.

She broke away, gasping for breath, but he dragged her back with a growl and they renewed the fight.

"Fuck me," she muttered, her teeth latching onto his lip once more. "God, please fuck me. Make this go away."

He gripped her hips, pulled her over his lap and her legs spread wide as he plunged into her depths. No hesitation, no preparation. Just straight, hard fucking. Her pussy was slick, hot, ready for him. As she straddled him, her knees tightened against his hips and she began riding his cock, pressing down on him with all the strength in her body. He bent forward, taking her breast into his mouth while his hands held her waist, lifting her, driving her back down.

The steam from the water surrounded them as it splashed over the sides of the Jacuzzi. They were stirring up a tidal wave—in and out of the tub. Drenching the floor. Drowning his heart. He didn't give a shit.

He'd clean up the mess. Somehow. Right now, he wanted more from her. So much more.

He bit her tight nipple and she cried out.

"Harder!"

He didn't know if she meant his cock or his teeth, so he delivered on both as she crash landed to earth with an orgasm that threatened to grind his cock to dust. He came with her, unable to fight back the pulsating grip of her pussy as it clenched against his turgid flesh. Pulse after pulse of hot come filled her, burning the tip of his dick as they continued to thrust, continued to pound into one another until every drop was spilled, every second filled with the racing thud of his heart.

And even then, he knew it wasn't enough.

## CHAPTER SIX

Wednesday…

Natalie brushed her hair, pinning it up in a ponytail. She and Ewan had returned from the hotel in time for him to work the lunch shift. She'd spent most of the afternoon hiding out in her room, trying to figure out what the hell she was supposed to do now. They'd taken a brief respite after the heated interlude in the Jacuzzi. When they'd woken up, Ewan had kissed her so tenderly, she'd known she was in trouble.

"Dammit," she muttered.

She didn't do this romance, Cupid, falling-in-love shit. It wouldn't work for her and last night solidified that fact. She'd told Ewan too much. If things continued to progress, there was no way she could keep him from discovering just how dark her world really was. She'd made it through this much of her life, succeeding in her career while avoiding messy relationships. She needed to find her way back to that.

"Knock knock."

Natalie looked up to find Teagan standing at her door and she was consumed with another emotion—guilt. She'd done a shitty job taking pictures for Sky's video. Ewan still had her little camera and aside from during the shopping trip yesterday, she hadn't touched her bigger cameras.

"Hey," Nat said, wishing she could invoke that tone of welcome that seemed second nature to Ewan.

"Hey yourself. You've been up here for hours, thought I'd check on you."

Natalie could see the curiosity on her friend's face. She'd been out all night with Teagan's brother—her *younger* brother. While the past week had all but erased the age difference in her mind, she wasn't sure how Ewan's family would feel about it.

*About what, Nat? You just had sex. That was all—sex.*

"I'm fine." Natalie's answer was forced, sharp, and she watched Teagan start to leave. She'd spent months at a time with this woman over the past three years, but they'd always struggled to make that one last connection toward friendship. Natalie knew it was her fault. Teagan had thrown more than a few planks of wood her way, trying to build a bridge. Natalie always used them for kindling.

"Teagan. Wait."

Teagan stepped back in the doorway.

"You got a minute?" Natalie swallowed uncomfortably. "To talk?"

Teagan grinned, coming in to join her. As they sat side by side on the bed, Natalie was reminded of spending more than a million days and nights like this with Yvonne. Chatting about boys, school, how lame their parents were…just life in general.

*In for a dime, in for a dollar*, Nat decided as she pointed out the elephant in the bedroom. "I spent the night with Ewan."

"I know."

"I…well, I'm not really seeking your approval for that or anything. I mean, I'm an adult and my personal life is just that. Personal." Natalie fought the impulse to close her eyes and groan. Where the hell had that nastiness come from?

Teagan merely laughed. "That didn't take long."

"What?" Natalie asked, confused by her response.

"Every now and then you invite me in, only to shut me right back out. I think today's effort may have eclipsed the previous record. How long have I been sitting here? Thirty seconds?"

Natalie stared at Teagan, feeling the crack in her wall start to rupture beneath the pressure. She was tired of being alone, keeping people at arm's length. She was confused as hell about her feelings and—

"I think Ewan is in love with me. With *me*," she repeated, showing her amazement at such a prospect. "He's handsome and kind and…God, I hope you don't hate me for this, but he's sexy as fuck and I can't, I don't…"

Teagan was quiet for only a moment before she prodded. "You don't what?"

"I don't know what to do with any of that. I don't have time for this love shit and besides, I live on the freaking west coast." She gestured around herself. "Um, hello? I'm not sure I can go any farther east than this."

Teagan grinned. "The Atlantic Ocean would probably stop you pretty quick."

She laughed at the joke briefly, and then closed her eyes. "He deserves better than me."

Teagan leaned back against the footboard of the bed and Natalie fought to hold her gaze, fought not to squirm.

"Aren't you going to say anything?" Natalie asked when the silence went on too long.

"I'm trying to put all this together in my head. You're the most confident woman I've ever met, Nat. You want something, you go after it, and I've never seen you question anything. Right or wrong, once you've made up your mind, you just start walking toward what you want."

"What's wrong with that?"

Teagan shook her head. "There's nothing wrong with that. I just worry that sometimes you push too hard and not always in the right direction."

Natalie took a deep breath, closing her eyes to say the next part. "I know Sky told you about my breakdown." She opened her eyes and looked at Teagan. "He told me."

Natalie was relieved to discover there wasn't any pity on her friend's face. Just compassion. Understanding.

"I hope you don't think he betrayed a trust there. Sky would never—"

Natalie held up her hand. "I'm not mad at him for telling you. Hell, you deserved to know why your boyfriend was constantly inviting another woman out on the road with the two of you. Sky seems to have a sixth sense. I don't know how he knows when I'm crashing, but he just does. Getting out of town usually helps."

"You're his best friend, Nat. He worries about you. He loves you."

"I'm glad he stuck around. A lot of people didn't. Not after…well, not after." Natalie hadn't talked this much about the blackest time in her life in years. Now within two days, she found herself spilling her guts to two different Collins siblings. She needed to get a grip on herself.

"You know, Sky's been calling every day asking about you. He's afraid hitting the road with us didn't help this time. I'm sort of starting to feel guilty. We haven't done much together this week apart from the shopping fiasco."

Natalie chuckled. "I think it's safe to say Riley would have you walking down the aisle in nothing but a thong and garter."

"I'm not taking her along the next time we go shopping. Jeez, can you believe the dresses she was picking out?"

"I don't know. I kind of like the black strapless number with the red lace." They laughed together. "Obviously Riley doesn't think much of the marriage institution."

Teagan sighed. "She doesn't think about much of

anything that doesn't include alcohol, loud music and late nights. I worry about her sometimes."

Natalie recalled her first night in Baltimore and hitting the clubs with Riley. Though the woman clearly enjoyed a party, she didn't ever get out of hand. Natalie suspected Aaron played a larger role in keeping Riley under control than anyone realized. "She's okay. My sister used to love a good party too. Some people are just born to socialize."

"Natalie, I'm just going to come out and say this. I admire you. If anything ever happened to one of my sisters, I don't know what I'd do."

"I wouldn't suggest a mental breakdown," Natalie said, her voice thick with the effort of making the jest.

"I'd fall apart and I would never be able to pull it back together. You did. You *have*."

Natalie wondered if that was true. She'd lived behind a wall of pain and guilt for years, suppressing the memories because thinking about them shredded her insides like a thousand knives. She'd buried herself in work, pushed away every friend she'd ever known except Sky, maintained the estranged relationship with her parents because it was easier than facing them and never allowed herself to fall in love because she didn't deserve happiness.

Didn't deserve to have a full, wonderful life when her sister couldn't have one too.

"You'd survive. You have Sky and your family. You're stronger than you think, though I pray to God you never have that strength tested."

"I hope so too. So I can tell Sky you're okay?" Teagan asked.

"I'm fine. I'm going back home on Saturday and I'm forging on—same as always. When are you going back on the road?"

"I think I might hang out here another week or two. Sky has more commitments than me. My big rock star," she said. Teagan's eyes shone with the love she felt for Sky and Natalie was happy they'd found each other. Opposites though they were, they fit.

"You'd have been passing Sky on the fame train if you'd put your mind to pursing your music career seriously, rather than hiding out here for years."

Teagan laughed. "You better not let Sky hear you say that. He's never said anything, but I've seen his face when a reporter chases us down and then asks me all the questions."

Natalie leaned forward, grinning widely. "That cocky sucker needed to be taken down a peg or two. You're good for him. You make him better simply by being with him. You sort of bring out his good side and temper his rougher edges."

"But his rough edges are still there," Teagan interjected.

"Of course, they are," Nat replied. "And thank God for that. That arrogance is a part of him. He wouldn't be Sky without it."

"No, he wouldn't, and I wouldn't love him if he weren't one hundred percent himself—bullheaded, conceited, sarcastic." They laughed at her words until

Teagan added, "Considerate, romantic…what was your description for Ewan? Sexy as fuck?"

Silence descended again, Ewan's name breaking the flow of the conversation and throwing Natalie back into her funk.

"How do you think Ewan would describe *you*?"

Natalie was taken aback by Teagan's question. "That's easy. Bitchy, opinionated, cynical."

"Where did you go last night?"

"Out to dinner at a fancy restaurant, swanky hotel room. Must have set him back at least a week's wages."

"Sounds romantic. Sounds like something a man would do to impress a woman he cares about." She grinned before adding, "Even if she *does* have a few rough edges."

Natalie didn't know how to respond. It was on the tip of her tongue to tell Teagan about the life lessons, but for some reason all of that seemed private, personal. Ewan had taken her out to teach her about romance, about letting go, letting herself have something she wanted without worrying about what it meant or why it mattered.

Last night the lesson had stuck, but this morning it had crumbled, shattered with the sunrise. It was that kiss as she woke up, the look in his eyes as he touched her face. He looked at her like she was beautiful, like she was special. One-night stands weren't all that unusual. She preferred them to sticky, committed relationships. Problem was, it hadn't felt like a one-night stand with Ewan. Not even close. And she desperately needed it to be a one-time thing. There was no way she could live with herself if she dragged Ewan down into the dark hole she called home. The more time she spent in his presence, the more she realized just how bad she would be for him.

Teagan had been silently watching her and she wondered what the other woman saw in her face.

"He's really gotten to you," Teagan said.

The self-protective shield flew up despite the fact she wanted to let Teagan in. She sucked at talking about emotions, so she fell back on what she knew—sarcasm. "He's been trying to get into my pants for three years. Last night he pulled out all the stops, caught me in a weak moment. Think it must have been the wine. It won't happen again."

Teagan clearly heard the dismissal in her voice and she stood. "That's a shame," she said when she reached the door. "I think you and Ewan are a perfect match."

Natalie watched her friend close the door behind her, that parting shot careening around in her head like a Ping-Pong ball. Perfect match? *No*, she wanted to yell out. *There's no match to be made here.*

Damn Sky Mitchell and his stupid birthday wish. He was the one who'd planted all this fluffy falling-in-love crap in her mind.

Damn Yvonne for dying on her when she needed someone to talk to.

Damn Teagan for making her think Ewan could love her for who she was—warts and all.

And damn Ewan for…

She fell back against her pillow and closed her eyes. Dammit all.

NATALIE ENTERED the pub shortly after ten. Ewan had left her alone most of the day, aware that last night's experience had thrown her for a loop. He'd hoped as the night passed they'd turned a corner in their budding relationship, but he could see now he'd hit the same brick wall again. Teagan had come down a few hours ago, said Natalie was confused. Then she'd actually warned him to tread lightly. Alluded to things in Natalie's past that he didn't know about and that he was inadvertently poking at some dark places by pursuing her. When Ewan pressed for more, Teagan told him it was Natalie's story to tell and walked away.

"Hiya, stranger," he said, walking over to greet her.

"Hey yourself." Her voice was strong, typical Nat, and he hoped that meant she'd made her peace with last night. Sadly, that peace seemed to have taken them right back to square one.

"Glad you made it down. I was just about to come drag you out of that room. We're running out of time on today's lesson."

Natalie put up her hand. "I don't want to play that game anymore, Ewan. It was a cute way to pass the time, but I've only got a couple more days here and I really wanted to get some pictures of Teagan and the wedding preparations for the photo-biography. Time is money."

"You agreed to a whole week. Seven lessons."

"I know what I agreed to, but it's a waste of time and now I'm bored with it. Move on, hotshot."

He narrowed his eyes. Natalie was pushing the wrong buttons tonight. He'd played the affable friend for years, letting her drive their relationship at a comfortable pace. The fact she lived on the other side of the country had held him back for most of their acquaintance, merely because time and distance were not on their side. This week had proven to him he'd been wrong to lay low, avoiding the obvious.

He wanted Natalie Miller, and he'd move heaven and earth to get her back in his bed and keep her there. Fuck the rest of it. They'd cross those bridges once they got there. *If* they got there.

"Well, if it's pictures you're after, I guess you'll want this back." He drew her camera out of his back pocket. She reached for it, but he pulled it back at the last minute.

"Give it to me," she demanded, holding out her hand.

He shook his head. "I'll give it back to you at the end of the night. At the end of the lesson."

"You have shitty hearing, Ewan. I told you—"

"I know what you told me but we're not finished. Not by a long shot. Now be a good girl. All we're going to do is sit at one of those tables over there. We're going to have a drink, listen to some karaoke and talk. That's it."

She gave him an angry smile. "Well, you see, that's the problem. I prefer the bad girl role, which means if you take this condescending attitude with me much longer, I'll cut your nuts off and shove them down your throat. Now give me back my camera."

Ewan laughed at her threat. God, she was a feisty thing when fired up. No doubt she'd intimidated men across the world with her fiery spirit. Pity of it was, it just drove his alpha male—the one he took care to hide—closer to the surface. "You've got the bad girl part all wrong. If you wanna be naughty, I'll throw you over my shoulder, take you up to your room, tie you to the bed and torment you with orgasms until you agree to finish the game."

"You know, that macho shit really doesn't work on me."

"Of course it does. Your nipples started poking through that shirt the second I said I was gonna tie you up. You into bondage, Nat? Because I'd love to hand-cuff you to a bed and—"

"You're gonna have to try to find a way off Fantasy Island soon, hotshot."

"What's it going to be? Good girl or bad girl?"

He watched her studying his face, trying to decide if he was bluffing. His cock was starting to strain against his jeans and he was seriously hoping she'd decide to test him. He took a step closer, ready to claim his naughty girl, but the movement must have clued her in and she held her hands up in surrender.

"I'm staying for the karaoke. I mean, that's why I came down here in the first place. Sean invited me."

He let her have the win and ushered her to a table. "Cool. It's the first night we're trying this. I think it's going to be a disaster but Sean swears it'll bring more people to the pub midweek. I'm not looking forward to hearing some of the performances."

"I personally can't wait to laugh my ass off," she replied, shuffling her chair slightly to face the stage. "Hate to admit it, but I'm a sucker for those *American Idol* auditions. Never miss them. The way some of those poor saps really think they can sing is too funny." Her shoulders relaxed a bit and he was relieved to see she was loosening up again. He released a soft sigh. For now, he'd let her play the friend card.

"You heartless woman," he said, chuckling. "I never miss them either. Offered to drive Teagan to New York to try out for one of the first seasons, but she just laughed at me."

"I can see you and Teagan standing in line for days just so Simon could call her a hippie and tell her she needed to change her image."

Ewan grinned widely. "You're probably right. But I bet he would have sent her on to Hollywood."

Nat agreed. "No question there. Oh my God, check out the guy in the purple cowboy shirt. Please tell me that's not fringe on the front."

Ewan looked toward the stage where she was pointing. "Oh yeah, definitely fringe. And snaps. Not a button on that beauty. Might have to ask him where he bought it."

"Don't you dare. Oh, and look. He's going to be the first singer." She gave Ewan a wicked grin. "This should be good."

The cowboy wannabe took the stage, propping himself on a stool and holding the microphone like he'd been born to it.

Natalie giggled softly. "Bet he sings into a hairbrush every morning," she whispered.

Ewan suspected she was right. The music began and the man started crooning an old Conway Twitty song that probably had the original singer spinning in his grave. Ewan looked over at Sean and raised his eyebrows as if to say, "I told you so."

Sean threw back a "look around" gesture and Ewan had to acknowledge the place was slowly and steadily filling up. Not a bad crowd for a Wednesday, actually. He conceded the point to his brother with a nod and struggled to block out the horrible singing emanating from the speakers. "This is borderline painful."

Natalie laughed. "I love it. Sean's a genius."

He looked at her, discovering she was sincere. "Never would have pegged you for a karaoke fan, Nat."

"I think everyone would like to spend five minutes in the spotlight. I've been around Sky enough over the last decade or so to know the feeling must be a rush like no other. His face when he finishes a concert is as close to bliss as I've ever seen."

Ewan wanted to say he'd seen that same look on *her* face last night when she came, but he kept the thought to himself. They'd forged an unsteady truce and he wasn't going to rock the boat...yet. "I'm glad you feel that way—because that's tonight's challenge."

"What?" she asked.

"I want you to get up on stage and sing."

She laughed hysterically, clearly thinking his words a joke until he added, "I dare you to sing a song, Nat."

She sobered up at the earnestness of his tone. "You can't be serious."

"I'm completely serious."

She fell silent for a moment and then grinned as if she'd found the magic loophole. "I will if you will."

"Fine," he answered easily, provoking a frown to cross her face. "But you go first."

She looked around and he sensed she was trying to find another way to escape the dare, so he threw more fuel on the fire. "Of course, if you're too afraid to get up there, I could always—"

"Where's the song list?" she asked, and he waved Sean over.

"What's up, bro?" Sean asked.

"Natalie wants to sing. Do you have one of those lists with the music selection?"

Sean quickly brought over a notebook filled with song choices and handed it to Natalie. "All right!" he said enthusiastically. "Way to keep the ball rolling, Nat. We're having a hard time getting folks to sign up. I owe you one." His brother bent down and gave her a friendly kiss on the cheek, the sweet gesture making her blush.

She studied the list for so long, Ewan feared she'd back out. He was surprised when she pointed and said, "This one."

He looked down and laughed. "Showing your age there, aren't you?"

"Bite me, Ewan. Go put my number in. And while you're at it, put yours in too. We had a deal. If I'm going to make an ass of myself, you're going down right alongside me."

He rose and turned in their two numbers. Sean grinned at his choice. "Duet?"

"Don't tell Natalie. I don't want her to have a chance to run."

Sean slapped him on the shoulder. "She's gonna kick your ass."

"Yeah, well, she seems to be on the verge of that every waking minute. It's sort of starting to lose its effect."

Sean laughed. "You got it bad for Sky's best friend."

Ewan considered denying it, but there wouldn't be any point. Of all his brothers, he was closest to Sean. Killian and Tris were twins and older, so that played a major role in the situation. Plus, Sean was just easy to be around.

"She's got my heart in her teeth. It's not a comfortable feeling."

"I guess not, although I don't see what the problem is. She's got the hots for you too."

Ewan considered that. "You think?"

"She hasn't left your side all week, bud."

"Yeah, well, that's actually because I've been working with her on something." Ewan wasn't sure why he didn't want to tell Sean about the life lessons, but something told him Nat wouldn't want anyone to know about her depression.

"Maybe so, but she can't take her eyes off you. Even now, she's checking out your ass."

Ewan grinned, but couldn't resist taking a peek over

his shoulder. Natalie's gaze was definitely on his southerly regions until she spotted him looking at her, then she quickly turned her head.

"She leaves in two days," he said, speaking the words that had been eating a hole in his gut all day. He was running out of time.

"So I guess you better kick it into high gear."

Ewan looked at his brother, his words striking a chord. "Yeah, I guess I better. Make sure you cue up her solo song first."

Sean grinned. "She's next. As soon as this guy finishes butchering Michael Jackson. I swear to God if he whips out the moonwalk, I might piss in my pants. This is even funnier than I thought it would be."

"Well, it's certainly brought in a crowd."

"Human nature," Sean said. "People are fascinated by tragedy."

Ewan shook his head, chuckling as he returned to the table. "Sean says you're up next."

"Great. You know, I think I failed to mention something."

"Oh yeah?" he asked. "What's that?"

"I can't sing."

"At all?" He was surprised by her confession. She had a lovely speaking voice, husky and sexy as hell. He just assumed that would translate to her being a pretty decent singer.

"Sky told me once he thought I might be tone deaf, but I can hear the melody, the harmony, everything that makes his songs great. I just can't make my voice do that."

He wondered why she wasn't more bothered by the prospect of getting on stage if she really did sing as bad as she said. "You're sure you're okay with getting up on the stage?"

"Turnabout's fair play," she said.

"Meaning?"

"Meaning," she leaned closer as she spoke, "I've spent years making fun of people for their shortcomings. I think maybe it's time I gave them a turn to take a few shots at me. Isn't that what this lesson is about?"

Ewan shook his head. "No, not at all. I was hoping you'd learn to stop caring what people think about you. You think the world hates you, sees you as a bitch. You pretend that doesn't bother you, but I think deep down inside, it does. This isn't about letting people laugh at you, Nat. I'd never set you up for that."

She sighed. "You are the most annoying man I've ever met."

"Why's that?"

"I find it very difficult to stay mad at you. And I really want to be mad at you right now."

He grasped her hand. "That's funny. I'm having some difficulties of my own in regards to you."

"What kind of difficulties?"

He pulled her hand into his lap, aware that the table was shielding them as he moved her palm to his very erect cock. "I really want to be inside you right now."

She started applying pressure to his cock, slowly moving her fingers along his covered flesh. "We already did the sex lesson." Her tone didn't match her words and he thought for a moment she was sad about the idea of not sleeping with him again.

"That wasn't a lesson, Nat. And I didn't intend for it to be just one night." Before he could say more, tell her exactly what the previous night meant to him, Sean was calling her name, gesturing for her to take the microphone.

She removed her hand and stood slowly. "Good."

"Good?" He was wondering how he could convince Sean to skip her in the line-up, but Natalie ignored his question and threw one of her own at him.

"You wanna know something?"

He nodded.

"I've always been jealous of Sky's time on the stage, in the spotlight. I've always wanted to try this just once and you're right, it doesn't matter what anyone else thinks. This is for me."

"Break a leg," he said, smiling at her sudden enthusiasm.

"But don't say I didn't warn you." She laughed as she walked away and Ewan watched her take her place on the stage, admiring her courage as she stood in the spotlight. As the music started, she held the microphone to her mouth and sang.

He covered his mouth to hide the grin emerging as she belted out Wilson Phillips' *Release Me*. Sean caught his eye and gave him a horrified look. She hadn't exaggerated about her singing. She looked at him as she continued, her twinkling eyes proving—unlike the *American Idol* wannabes—she knew exactly how bad she sounded.

Regardless of the sound, she was winning the crowd over with sheer showmanship. As the pace of the song increased, she started dancing, her motions sultry and beautiful, despite her singing. She started working the crowd, pointing to a few of the men, who began wolf-whistling. Their enjoyment pushed her further and he broke into genuine laughter when she left the stage and started singing to the cowboy in the purple shirt, playing with his fringe.

The crowd was eating up her antics and a few women stood up and started singing along. Apparently, she'd stumbled upon some sort of '90s girl anthem. Everyone started clapping, dancing at their seats, and Sean turned to give him a thumbs-up.

As the song ended, she received the first standing ovation of the night and she ran back to the table where he stood waiting for her. She hugged him, laughing with complete, unrestrained joy and, as everyone watched and cheered louder, he kissed her.

"That was so awesome," she said when they broke apart.

"And you said you couldn't sing." He kept his hands on her hips, even though he caught Tris and Pop looking at him from behind the bar. His family had suspected something was up between them, but he had a feeling the kiss he'd just given her in front of God and everyone had laid any lingering doubts to rest.

"Very funny." She was still grinning, still on a karaoke high.

"What do you say we try to get an encore out of the

lovely Miss Natalie?" Sean said from the stage, the crowd cheering on his suggestion.

She started to shake her head when Sean held up a slip of paper. "As luck would have it," he said, "I happen to have Natalie all lined up for a duet with none other than my brother, Ewan."

There were enough regulars in the crowd that Ewan wasn't surprised by the hearty applause and encouragement. No doubt they were looking forward to seeing him make an ass of himself.

"That wasn't the deal," she exclaimed, but he could tell by her face she wasn't angry.

"Guess I've never really shared this spotlight dream of yours. Unless you're sharing it with me."

She smiled. "I want to sleep with you again."

His heart started racing at her admission. He could tell it was hard for her to say the words. "Good." She rolled her eyes as he threw her word back at him and they made their way to the stage together.

As they took their places on the stools, she looked at him. "I forgot to ask. What are we singing?"

"*I Got You Babe.*"

She closed her eyes and for a moment, he thought she was praying she'd heard him wrong. When she opened them again, they were filled with laughter. "Sonny and Cher? You know, now that I look at you, you do favor—"

"Nat," he warned with feigned anger. The music started. "Shut up and sing."

They made it through the song without embarrassing themselves. Actually, once they started singing, he found that the people sitting around them disappeared because his eyes were focused solely on her. She did a better job with Cher, though she struggled to find at least half the notes. It was hard to notice or care because she was having so much fun. At one point, she swung her hair over her shoulder in true Cher style and Ewan heard Pop cheering her on from the bar. His pop was a sucker for the old *Sonny and Cher Show*.

Fortunately Natalie had already won over the crowd so they were generous with their applause, and as they left the stage, several men rose to slap him on the back. Apparently she'd stolen some hearts and at least two of the patrons told him he was a lucky bastard.

They went back to their table and Pop carried over a couple of beers. "Thought you two might have worked up a thirst after all that singing."

Natalie giggled. "Thanks, Pat."

"You made a fine Cher, Natalie. Sunday and I used to watch their show on television every week. Ewan, I must admit I'm surprised. Didn't know you could sing like that."

Pop looked around and did a quick survey of the tables before joining them. Ever the attentive barman. Ewan suspected his pop knew exactly how many minutes he could sit and chat before someone would need a refill.

Ewan chuckled, but Natalie and Pop looked at him seriously. "You sounded awesome," she added. "Amazing, actually."

He brushed off their praise, but Pop wasn't content to let the subject lie. "My kids get their singing talent from Sunday. She had a beautiful voice. Used to sing you to sleep every night, Ewan. Remember?"

Ewan tried to swallow past the lump in his throat.

"She had a song for each kid. Sang it to them when they were babies right on up until they were starting school. Usually by the time they were three or four, they'd be singing right along. I used to stand in the hall some nights and listen as she sang the kids to sleep. Such a voice."

Ewan knew not a day passed that his pop didn't miss his mom. He wondered what it must feel like to have such a deep and undying love. He glanced at Natalie and felt his heart twinge. His gut and his heart told him she was the one. If anyone could provoke those emotions, bring his life that kind of complete and unending happiness, it would be her. Now he just had to convince Natalie.

"What was the song she used to sing to you, Ewan? I can't remember."

Ewan was jerked from his thoughts by his pop's unexpected question. Song? He licked his suddenly dry lips and took a drink of beer to stall, his mind racing for an answer.

"*Beautiful Boy*," Pop shouted out at last. "That was it. Sunday had a terrible crush on John Lennon. I think that song came out a few years before you were born. She loved it, sang it to you all the time. She never admitted as much, but I sort of suspect she stole the name Sean from Lennon and Yoko Ono's son."

Pop chuckled at the memory, but Ewan had stopped listening as a tune started to form in his mind.

Before he could think better, he found himself singing the song. "Life is what happens to you while you're busy making other plans." He smiled as he realized he knew all the words. If he hadn't been so overwhelmed by the thought, he could have sung every verse right there, though he hadn't heard the song since…

He remembered, heard his mother's voice in his head. The memory as clear as if she'd sung it to him yesterday. He swallowed, trying to dislodge the lump in his throat.

A memory.

"Yep, that's the song. You've got Sunday's talent," Pop said as he rose, grinning delightedly. "Well, back to work. You two gonna give the karaoke another whirl tonight?"

Natalie shook her head. "Nope. I think I've already exhausted my five minutes of fame."

Pop walked away to take the drink orders of a couple who'd just come in as Ewan watched, not really paying attention.

"That's a far-away look." Natalie's gaze was intent on his face.

"Just thinking about my mom."

"You miss her."

He looked at her. "Yeah, I do."

Natalie leaned closer as if to comfort him and he was driven by the impulse to kiss her. Really kiss. Kiss her until she had no choice but to admit what he already knew. He was tired of playing games, tired of pretending. Tonight, the shields came down.

"Come upstairs with me."

She tried to move away slightly but he grasped her hands and drew her closer, not allowing her retreat. "You said you wanted to sleep with me again."

"I know what I said, but sometimes doing what you want *isn't* a good thing." She was purposely contradicting the previous night's lesson.

"Why?"

"Because sex just muddies the water."

He frowned. "Stop doing this, Nat. Dammit, every step forward with you is followed by twelve back. Stop thinking. Stop hiding. Wallow in the mud with me."

"Your family—"

"Knows about us. I think they'd have to blind at this point not to see what's going on."

"And they won't mind you spending the night in my bed?" She glanced over her shoulder, looking at Pop as he took another drink order.

He pulled her face back to look at him, his fingers gripping her chin. "I'm an adult. You're an adult. Besides, didn't we just spend tonight going over the concept of not worrying about what other people think? Do you want to be with me?"

"God. Yes."

"Then come upstairs. Let me make—"

She placed a finger on his lips, halting him, refusing to hear the word *love*, and he felt his anger, his frustration build.

"Whether I say it or not, it's still there, Nat. You know it and I know it."

She shook her head, pressing her forehead against his. "I really need you to stop talking."

He laughed. "Wearing you down, aren't I?"

She grinned and rose. "Come on."

He took her proffered hand and started humming *I Got You Babe*. By the time they reached the stairs leading to the apartment, he started singing the words to her as she giggled. "I've got you to hold my hand. I've got you to understand."

# CHAPTER SEVEN

Thursday…

Natalie woke up for the second day in a row with her head pillowed on Ewan's chest. She tried not to acknowledge how comfortable the position was. A quick glance at the clock proved it was still early—not quite seven. She should be sleeping the sleep of the dead after the night she'd just spent. Apparently Ewan was a big fan of foreplay—not that she had a problem with foreplay. He'd kissed and caressed her for what felt like hours until every nerve in her body was screaming for more. He was an excellent lover, generous, attentive. It didn't hurt that he was well endowed, either. She loved the way he filled her.

She wondered what he tasted like. Peering up, she confirmed he was asleep and she decided revenge, in this instance, could be very, very sweet. She slowly pushed herself away from his body, relieved when he didn't stir. She pulled the covers off, admiring the view along the way. She was surprised to discover him already half-erect and she glanced at his face again. He was definitely still asleep. She wondered what he was dreaming about.

Kneeling by his right hip, she bent down. She could detect the slightest scent of their lovemaking from the night before. She paused, regrouped. Not lovemaking. Sex. *Sex.*

"Sex," she whispered against his cock. As she spoke, his erection grew more prominent.

"Sex sounds good," he murmured, his voice husky with sleep.

She grinned when she spotted his gaze on her. Rather than answer, however, she ran her tongue along his hard shaft, from root to tip.

He hissed as she hovered at the slit, lapping up the pre-come already gathering there. She remembered the night in the Jacuzzi, how much his rough touches enflamed her. She wondered if she could provoke the same response in him. With that thought in mind, she nipped the head of his cock. Sank her teeth in and tried not to gloat at his jerky response.

"Easy, babydoll. I've kind of grown fond of that cock. We've been together for twenty-six years. I'd hate for anything to happen to the poor guy."

She giggled, pulling her teeth away and sucking the mushroom head into her mouth as she reached to grip his balls.

He groaned. "That's much better. Dammit! I love the way you wake up."

She took him deeper as she squeezed his scrotum.

His hands flew to her hair, his fingers tangling in her tresses, pulling lightly. She squirmed at the impact of it. She had no idea how erotic hair pulling could be. Her thighs were damp with her arousal, amazed at Ewan's ability to bring her to this point so quickly.

She moved lower on his cock, trying to take as much as she could. Using her free hand, she gripped the flesh she couldn't quite squeeze into her mouth. His cock brushed the back of her throat and she swallowed.

Ewan jerked beneath her. "Holy fuck. Jesus, Nat."

She moved back then repeated the action. Over and over, she took him deep, swallowing the head until he was thrashing, fighting to restrain his reactions.

"God dammit! I can't last like this. It's too good. Ah, babydoll. You are so hot, so sweet."

His grip on her hair tightened and she knew he was getting close. She released his balls and ran her finger along his perineum, placing her fingertip at his anus as she swallowed his cock once more.

The single touch fired him like the trigger of a gun. "God yes," he cried as he came in her mouth. "Swallow it, Natalie. Take it all, baby."

She held him in her mouth as his climax subsided. Simply held him there, lightly running her tongue over his softening flesh. He stroked her hair absentmindedly for several moments as she tried to understand her uncharacteristic compulsions when it came to him. She'd never wanted to give a guy a blowjob, had rarely done it in the past. The action was more a chore, a payback of sorts after a lover went down on her. She wasn't used to *wanting* to give in the bedroom, more than she wanted to take. Sex was to fulfill a need—that was it.

So why was she laying on a bed with Ewan's cock in her mouth, not giving a shit if he returned the favor?

She was happy because *he* was happy. That couldn't be normal.

"Come here," he said gruffly, reaching under her arms to pull her to his side. When they were face-to-face, he gave her another one of those magical kisses. It was deep and strong and felt like so much more than a mere merging of lips. He was fucking with her head and she was letting him.

His hand drifted to her aching pussy and she cried out at the first touch of his finger on her swollen clit. He pulled away from her mouth and looked at her. Simply watched her face as his fingers continued to play, his strokes coming faster, stronger, going deeper.

He pushed her onto her back. "Open your legs."

Her knees fell apart as two fingers speared into her vagina. "Ewan," she whispered, loving the sound of his name.

"I'm right here."

She gripped his shoulders as he worked his fingers into her sheath, each thrust driving her higher than she'd ever imagined flying. She groaned when he rose up and knelt between her legs. His hot breath on her pussy branded her, the added sensation killing her with pleasure. He took her clit between his teeth and she was reminded of the nip she'd just given his cock. His tongue explored her mons while his fingers maintained their relentless, glorious pounding.

She was on the brink of a climax, but knew it wouldn't be enough. "No," she said, grasping his wrist, trying to halt his lovely assault. "You. I want you. Inside me."

He looked like he wanted to protest and she wondered for a moment if it was too soon. He had just come. Her worries were swept away when he rose on his knees, his erection riding thick and high against his stomach.

"Roll over," he said, lifting her hips, turning her until she was on her hands and knees in front of him. "I want to go deeper. So deep I get lost. I never want to find my way out again."

She shivered at his sensual words. Her heart inviting him in, luring him into the darkest depths, determined to hide him from her fucked-up head.

She looked over her shoulder and grinned. "So get lost."

He groaned as her familiar taunt took on new meaning. Gripping her hips, he pushed himself into her so slowly, she wanted to scream. She fought to press back against him, determined to speed up his pace, but his hands held her fast, holding her hostage to his will.

"Ewan," she said, her fists gripping the sheets in the face of his torment.

"Not yet."

Onward he pressed until he was finally—finally—buried to the hilt. He stopped for a moment, bending forward, his lips grazing the skin at the nape of her neck. "You belong here, Nat. With me. Always with me." His whispered words resonated too strongly and her throat seized up on her reply.

Ewan didn't seem to notice as he continued. "If you would just crack a window in that heart of yours, you would see the truth."

She shook her head once, trying to ward off his words.

"I'm going to prove it. I'm going to take you now. Take you hard enough to shake the rafters, crumble your foundation."

She was trembling, fear laced with an unbearable lust. If anyone could drag her from her self-imposed exile, it was Ewan.

He didn't wait for a response. He merely pulled his cock out until just the head was seated inside her opening. And then he took her, just as he said he would.

She gasped as he pummeled his way into her body, into her heart. His hands tightened on her waist and it was all she could do to hold on to the bed. As he thrust, he showered her with words—beautiful, powerful words of love, of lust, of need and desire. He shattered her resistance as his motions sped up, quicker, harder.

"God, yes," she cried.

Reaching around her, he pressed his fingers against her clit. She trembled as he provoked a landslide of sensation and she felt herself tumbling, plummeting toward the ground. She expected to smash with the impact but as her orgasm took her, Ewan's arms enveloped her, held her as she shook, and she knew no matter what happened, he'd catch her.

His movements never ceased. She was caught up in

a whirlwind, her senses on overload as she tried to process his words, savor the smell of their combined juices—sex and sweat had never seemed so potent. Her skin was almost painful to the touch and yet that's what he continued to do, rubbing her arms with his rough palms, caressing her back with kisses then nipping at her shoulders with his teeth while holding her legs open with the firm press of his knees. His strong touches told her she'd never be denied, never be turned away.

He continued his thrusting as a second climax built.

"Come with me this time," she cried. "Don't wanna be alone."

He tightened his hold, plunged deeper, and when she came again his groans mixed with hers and they fell to the mattress in an exhausted heap of naked, sweaty body parts. Natalie loved the feeling of his legs tangled with hers, his arms wrapping around her chest like a vise. She didn't want him to let go, but she didn't know how to ask him to stay. How could she ask him to take a chance on her?

For several moments they were quiet. Natalie was surprised to discover she'd drifted back to sleep. When she opened her eyes again, Ewan was pulling the sheet over her chilled body. She turned in his arms, uncertain of her emotions, her words. As she looked up, he smiled. The same crooked smile. And she knew she didn't have to say a thing. It was Ewan. He knew her. Knew her and accepted her.

He bent down and kissed her, one soft, almost platonic kiss. "I have to get ready for work. I'm on the lunch shift again."

"I'm going down to the waterfront today with Teagan and your pop. There's a florist down there she wanted to check out and I wanted to get some pictures of them by the Bay. Sean's going to come along and be our muscle."

Ewan laughed. "Still can't get used to Teagan getting mobbed by fans."

"It's not that bad for her. Yet. She's making more of a name for herself with the songwriting than the singing, though her singing career isn't going so bad. Sky has it worse because, much as it pains me to say this, women are insane when it comes to rock stars."

"Yeah, I've witnessed some of that insanity these past few years. I don't know how he can stand the screaming and crying and grabbing."

Natalie stretched onto her back, marveling at how natural it felt to lie in bed and talk to Ewan. No matter where they were, what they were doing, he was simply easy to be with.

"You know, parking is expensive downtown. Why don't you guys cab it to the waterfront and I'll pick you up after the lunch shift? There's a really nice park on the outskirts of town you might like. You could take some photographs there and then we'll all go out to dinner."

Her mind was already thinking of all the pictures she'd love to take of Ewan. With his dark hair and eyes, his chiseled jaw, she knew he'd be a wonderful model. She'd love to shoot him in black and white. Her mind's eye started creating the set-ups she'd use.

"Uh oh. I don't like the way you're looking at me

right now." His head was propped up on his hand, his elbow supporting the weight. His hair was tousled from sleep and her fingers. He was breathtakingly handsome.

"I'd love to shoot you."

He grinned. "That's nothing new."

"Take photographs of you," she clarified with a laugh.

"I'd rather you hand the camera off to someone else and let them take pictures of us."

Her heart gave a funny lurch at the thought. "Of us?"

"Why not? You're gorgeous. I'd love to have a picture of the two of us together. I could sleep with it under my pillow. Pull it out like a dirty magazine when I'm—"

She punched him in the gut as he laughed. "You filthy pervert," she teased, picking up her pillow and hitting him in the head with it. He threw up his hands to protect himself as she continued to swing it at him.

He captured her hand, tossing the pillow off the bed before pushing her back on the bed, coming over her to cage her in. "I'd much rather have the real thing in my bed," he said, kissing her. His cock nudged her thigh and she opened her legs, wrapped them around his waist as he entered her in one swift, marvelous plunge.

"God," she cried, when he rocked against her. "I can't get enough of you. Of *this*."

His lips rasped her neck, his teeth lightly biting her

shoulder. She quivered at the impact, her pussy throbbing at his delicious prodding.

Her hands clung to his neck as she tightened her legs, using them to pull him into her—faster, harder.

"Dammit, Nat. I can't, I want—"

"Give it to me. Please, Ewan. Fill me up. I'm tired of being empty."

He reached down and stroked her clit, rolling the pearl between his fingers until she screamed, the rush, the release too powerful to contain any longer.

His dick surged into her one last time before he came. And as he kissed her, she wondered how a person could feel lost and found all at the same time.

NATALIE SAT ON A BENCH, people watching and resting. She'd spent a full, busy afternoon with Teagan, Sean and Pat and she had to admit, the longer she spent with the Collins family, the more she liked them. They were genuine, goodhearted and fun. It had been a long time since she'd been with her family like this— the entire structure of her own home falling apart with Yvonne's death and her stint in the mental hospital. She'd forgotten how special family was and she was gripped with regret for letting hers go without a fight.

She glanced at her watch. Ewan had called forty-five minutes earlier to say he was leaving the pub. She knew from the cab ride here, the trip—even with traffic—shouldn't have taken more than fifteen minutes.

"I can't understand what's taking Ewan so long,"

Teagan said for the fifth time. "We should have just gotten a cab back to the pub and left from there."

"That would have been too much backtracking. We just have to come back this way to get to Winter Park." Sean was leaning against a light pole, his eyes watching the traffic behind her, looking out for Ewan's car.

"Yeah, well. If he'd answer his phone, we could tell him to forget the park. I'm beat." Teagan was clearly as worn out as her, and Natalie had to agree the idea of going one more place today after all the walking they'd done this afternoon, traveling from shop to shop, was last on her list of fun ideas. She'd prefer to take a nice, long soak in the bathtub with a glass of wine and Ewan.

The thought reminded her again of the Jacuzzi and she grinned at the memory of straddling his hips and drawing him into her—

"I hope nothing happened to him." Pat's comment jarred her from her naughty thoughts and for the first time, she felt a touch of panic. What if something *had* happened to him?

"He would have called," Sean replied.

If he could. The idea that Ewan wouldn't be able to call them suddenly terrified her. She stood up and stared down the street, her heart racing at the thought he could be injured, hurt…worse.

She opened her cell phone and dialed his number again. She'd tried several times in the last hour, as had Teagan, but the thing kept sending her to voicemail. As she heard his recorded voice asking her to leave a message, Teagan's phone rang. She clicked hers shut and turned anxiously toward Ewan's sister.

"It's Keira," Teagan said with a sigh, opening her cell. "Hey, sis. What's up?"

Teagan was quiet for a moment. "Is he okay?"

The question sent a surge of ice water pumping through Natalie's veins and her knees gave way as she dropped back onto the bench.

"Which hospital?" Teagan asked.

"Ewan's in the hospital?" Sean stepped closer but Teagan raised her hand for him to be quiet.

"Okay. Yeah. We'll just get cab. No problem." Teagan clicked her phone closed and looked at her pop. "Ewan was in a car accident right outside the pub. Some teenager who just got his license. Ran a red light, plowed into the side of his Subaru."

"Driver's side?" Sean asked, and Teagan nodded.

Natalie struggled to hear the rest of her words but there was a sudden, painful roar of thunder pulsing through her ears, deafening her. She clenched her hands into fists to stop the uncontrollable shaking taking over her body.

Teagan's next words sounded like they were coming to her through a tunnel, their sound muffled, garbled. "He's okay, but the rescue squad came and took him to the hospital. Apparently he's got a nasty gash on his head that needed stitches and they're concerned about a concussion. He's also got some bad bruises on his left leg."

Natalie licked her dry lips, tried to focus, but the spots forming behind her eyes alerted her to the coming panic attack. She hadn't had one in years. Never let herself get this upset, this distressed. She started rocking.

"Nat," Sean said quietly. "You okay? You're white as a sheet."

She tried to get a breath but it felt like the air wasn't getting to her lungs.

"Jesus, Natalie." Sean's tone told her exactly how crazy she looked. "Put your head between your knees. You look like you're gonna pass out."

She let him push her head down as she continued to struggle to breathe. For several long minutes, she tried to close down everything—the worried whispers of Ewan's family, the sounds from the people walking by, the horns blaring in the midday traffic. She put it all away, as she'd learned to do in the past, and simply listened to her breathing.

In and out. She focused on the rush of it as it came into her lungs then left her body again.

She wasn't sure how much time had passed, but she was pulled out of her trance by Sean's hand on her back. "Natalie? Do you think you can get in the cab? We want to get you home and in bed. You don't look so good."

Natalie slowly sat up, exhaustion setting in. "I'm okay," she whispered.

"Pop's flagged down a taxi. He's waiting at the curb. Think you can walk? If not, I can carry you."

A weak smile crossed her lips at his gallant offer. He was so much like Ewan…

The thought of Ewan sent a fresh round of panic through her body. "Ewan's okay?"

Sean smiled, though his face betrayed his worry. "I have a feeling he's beat us home. He'll be there when we get back."

She took his proffered hand and stood, leaning heavily on him as she walked to the cab.

During the ride home, no one spoke, no one asked her any questions and she was glad for their consideration. She'd fallen apart in front of them. She knew she'd be mortified later, but right now all she could think about was Ewan.

He'd been in a car accident. He could have been killed. She would have lost him.

Lost him like she'd lost Yvonne.

She didn't know what to do with the pain suffusing her, where to put it. She'd held people at bay for years, managed her illness by keeping them out.

"We're here, Nat." She glanced up, surprised to see everyone had stepped out of the taxi. She followed them into the pub, her eyes scanning the crowd for Ewan.

Tris waved to them as they entered and she could see he was puzzled by the somberness of their small group of four. "Didn't Keira tell you he's okay? He's upstairs, pissed as hell about the dent in his car."

Teagan nodded. "We know he's okay. Natalie's not feeling well. Must've been something we ate for lunch."

Natalie was grateful for Teagan's lie and Sean's arm as they continued through the bar to the stairs to the apartment above. As they reached the top, Natalie saw

Keira and Will sitting on the couch in the living room, Catie on the floor, glued to *Sesame Street* on the television.

Ewan was on his cell, pacing around the dining room table and arguing with someone about insurance.

Natalie stopped at the top of the stairs and stared at him, studied his face, worried about the bruises, the bandage at his brow, the way he was limping slightly. As the rest of the family moved into the room, he saw her and his words stopped.

"I'll call you back later," he said, hanging up abruptly.

The room was eerily quiet given the number of people gathered there. "Hey, Nat." His voice was the same…friendly, open, though she could hear the underlying thread of tiredness there. "Sorry about our plans."

She tried desperately to find her voice and failed. He was here. He was okay.

He could have died.

"I…" She cleared her throat. "I have a headache. I need to go lie down."

For the first time, Ewan seemed to *see* her. He noticed Sean standing by her arm, ready to catch her, and he spotted the worried looks on Pat's and Teagan's faces.

She tried to pull her gaze away from his face, tried to ignore the implosion racking through her body. "Thank you, Sean." Her voice sounded rusty, rough. "I can make it to my room just fine."

She turned, praying her legs would carry her the

ten steps to the foot of the stairs leading to the third floor, begging her body to lift her up the fourteen steps to the landing. Every eye was on her, she knew.

She couldn't let them see. Couldn't let them know.

Ewan was by her side before she took the first step. "Nat?"

She could hear the question in his voice, the concern. "Just a little headache. I'll take some aspirin and sleep. I'll be fine." She looked at him then, because she simply couldn't resist checking one more time, making sure for herself. "I'm glad you're okay, Ewan."

His puzzled face crushed the tiny part of her heart that refused to stop beating, refused to stop living. She forced a smile to her lips but she knew it didn't fool him. Determination ran strong in him and she knew he wouldn't let her go without an explanation. Unfortunately she didn't have one to give him.

"Please," she pleaded quietly.

"I'll help you up the stairs," he said, but she shook her head.

"Your leg—"

"Is fine. Come on. Just up the stairs." His tone told her she would get her reprieve. He wouldn't make her talk, not now, but that was the only point he was conceding. He took her arm and she closed her eyes at his gentle strength. She'd been leaning on it too much this week.

No more.

They climbed the stairs under the watchful eyes of his family. At the doorway to her room, she stopped. "Thank you." Her face, her words let him know he was dismissed, and he narrowed his eyes angrily. She thought he might insist on seeing her in. She knew the caretaker in him wanted to put her in bed, tuck her in, hold her in his arms until he was sure she was okay.

She refused to budge. Refused to let him in. If she let him in now, she'd never be able to let him go—and she *had* to let him go.

"You should get some rest too," she added. "I'll see you in the morning." She turned and walked in, relieved when he didn't follow her. She refused to turn to look at him as she quietly closed the door and locked it.

EWAN CAME DOWN the stairs as Keira and Will were taking their leave. "Glad you're okay, baby brother," Keira said as she planted a kiss on his brow. "I'm gonna see Will and Catie off and then I'll take care of the dinner shift. You get some rest."

"Will do. Thanks for everything today, Kiki." His sister had just been arriving at the restaurant when the car accident occurred. Her steady presence had gone a long way toward calming Riley, who was threatening to beat the shit out of the poor kid driving the other car. She'd gone to the hospital with him, filled out the mountains of paperwork and made him laugh while the doctor put in the stitches. In short, she was an awesome big sister.

He kissed Catie goodbye, shook hands with Will and watched them descend the stairs. Once they were gone, he turned to face Teagan, Sean and Pop. "Anybody wanna tell me what the fuck happened to Nat?"

"Sit down, Ewan." He could tell by Pop's calm voice—and the fact his father didn't scold him for his language—he wasn't going to like what they had to say.

He sat on the couch next to Teagan and braced himself. He'd never seen Nat look so... Damn, he couldn't think of a word for what had been on her face just now. A million things were displayed there and none of them had looked good—terror, depression, anger, sadness, sickness. Despite all the warring emotions, rather than cry, scream or lash out, she'd stood there like a statue. Like she had to think about every breath she took, every word she said, every step she made. It was the single-most frightening thing he'd ever witnessed.

"So?" he prompted.

"She sort of..." Teagan paused.

"Fell apart." Sean propped himself on the coffee table in front of him while Pop claimed the recliner.

"Fell apart?" he asked.

"Keira called and I guess Natalie heard that you'd been in a car accident, that you were in the hospital—" Teagan stopped when Ewan interrupted her.

"Yvonne," he whispered.

She nodded.

"Who's Yvonne?" Sean asked.

"Natalie's sister was killed in a car crash about ten years ago. They were best friends." Ewan didn't add that Natalie blamed herself for the accident.

Sean leaned forward, his elbows on his knees. "No wonder she flipped out."

"It was more than that, Sean." Pop sat forward in his chair and Ewan could see his father was worried. "It was more than her just being worried or upset. If I'm not mistaken, she suffered a full-blown panic attack. Her color, her breathing, her trembling. It was too pronounced, too much. I was concerned we'd be following you to the hospital, Ewan. But then she pulled it together. It was like she knew exactly what to do to steady herself."

Teagan sat back and sighed, and Ewan looked at her. "You know something. You've alluded to it before."

His sister glanced uneasily at Pop and his father rose from the chair.

"Come on, Sean. Let's go downstairs and see if Keira and Tris need help."

"But I'm off tonight," Sean protested.

Pop chuckled and slapped Sean lightly on the shoulder. "Ah son, there are times when you just need an excuse to make a graceful exit. This is one of them."

Sean looked from Teagan to Ewan, and then sighed. "If you wanted me to go away, you just had to say so."

Ewan looked at him and smiled. "Go away."

"Sorry about your car, bro. I'm glad you're okay," Sean said as he stood.

"Thanks, Sean."

Ewan watched his pop and Sean disappear down the staircase to the pub below and then he turned to face his sister. Her brow was furrowed and he could tell she was fighting her conscience. His heart sank as he wondered what the secret she'd been keeping from him could be.

"Teagan, please."

"What I know, Ewan, it was told to me in confidence. I don't think I should—"

"What is it, Teagan?" He felt his temper rising. Natalie was lying upstairs alone after locking him out again. All the progress he'd made this week lay shattered around his feet.

Teagan closed her eyes for a moment before opening them again and looking him straight in the eye. "She had a nervous breakdown after her sister's death. She spent nearly six months in a mental hospital. Since then, she's suffered slight setbacks, never anything as serious as the first one. She battles depression. She battles it hard, according to Sky. It's like she won't let herself admit any worry, any sadness. To avoid it, she's sort of closed herself off from people."

Every word Teagan said was drawing a clearer picture in his mind of the woman Natalie had become after her sister's death—and he suddenly realized exactly what he was up against.

The wall he thought he'd scaled to reach her had just turned into a mountain. And he was stranded in the valley.

# CHAPTER EIGHT

F riday…

Natalie escaped the apartment a little after dawn. She'd tossed and turned all night in her attempts to block out the day's events. When she'd finally drifted off, her dreams had turned on her as visions of Yvonne and Ewan, both battered and bloody, lay amongst the crushed metal of a car. She'd awoken sweaty and trembling, too terrified to close her eyes again.

She walked aimlessly around Baltimore for hours, her thoughts such a jumble of images and emotions, her tired mind eventually just shut down. She meandered around the streets like a zombie, avoiding the restaurant…and Ewan.

As the morning became afternoon, she shook herself from her melancholy and dug deep, trying to find the strength to do what she knew came next. She'd been a fool to tempt fate, to succumb to Ewan's charming advances. Love wasn't for her. She wasn't a good bet. She was nothing but a walking, talking, emotional wreck…and Ewan deserved a hell of a lot better than her. Christ. He was optimistic, cheerful, happy. All those traits and emotions she fucking sucked at.

Besides, she'd been to hell because of caring for someone and she wasn't about to go back there. She didn't care if she was alone, restless, in a funk. All of that was preferable to the pain she'd felt yesterday and last night as she imagined Ewan dying.

As she turned back toward Pat's Pub, she knew two things beyond the shadow of a doubt. She was strong enough to walk away. She *wasn't* strong enough to stay.

The sun was beginning its descent when she walked into Sunday's Side. The dinner rush was just starting and as soon as the scent of Riley's cooking hit her nose, her stomach rumbled and she realized she hadn't eaten since lunchtime the day before.

Ewan spotted her before she'd made it two steps in the door. "Where the hell have you been?"

His annoyed tone piqued her anger. "Out walking."

"All day?"

She put her hands on her hips, grateful for his attitude. She knew how to fight. She thrived on arguments, found herself in anger. She preferred it to heart-to-heart talks and fucking pity. "I didn't realize I was on a schedule here. I sort of thought this was *my* vacation and I could do whatever the hell I pleased."

Ewan didn't back down and she thought she'd managed to spark a little bit of Mr. Easy-going Ewan's temper. It felt good. "You weren't feeling well last night.

I don't think it's that difficult to believe I'd be worried when you went missing this morning. Jesus, Nat. I called every fucking hospital."

She tried not to let his concern, his sweet gesture get to her. He'd called every hospital? For her? She pushed the thought out and scrambled to regain her momentum. "I'm not your responsibility."

Her words hit him harder than if she'd slapped him. She could see it, and she turned her head, refusing to look at the hurt in his eyes.

"Is that right?" His tone was cold.

"This conversation is becoming tedious. I need to go upstairs and pack. I'm leaving tomorrow morning, you know." She tried to step around him but he caught her upper arm in a grip tighter than she'd ever felt. Usually he was so gentle, so careful with her. She wasn't accustomed to feeling his real strength. "Let go of me."

He shook his head and then glanced at their surroundings. She followed his gaze around the room. They were attracting an audience. "I only need a moment of your time. My office." Then because she narrowed her eyes, ready to lambaste him, he added a "please." While his body was stiff, his posture almost aggressive, his eyes were softer, pleading.

"Five minutes," she said, knowing she was about to live through the longest three hundred seconds of her life.

She followed him into his office, trying to hide the alarm on her face when he locked the door. "Is that necessary?" she asked.

"I don't want us to be interrupted." He leaned back against the door as she snorted.

"You don't want me to escape. Clock's ticking, hotshot." She looked at her watch. "Four minutes and forty-five seconds."

"I love you."

She froze, certain she couldn't have heard his words correctly. "What?"

"I love you. I'm in love with you."

She opened her mouth, fought for an answer, tried to regain the confidence she'd spent all afternoon wrapping around herself.

"Don't be ridiculous," she whispered.

Ewan chuckled mirthlessly. "Ridiculous. First time in my life I tell a woman I'm in love with her and she thinks it's ridiculous."

"I don't mean…I'm not saying you're…" She fought to find a way out, a loophole. "You don't know me. There are things, Ewan—"

"I know you had a nervous breakdown. I know you suffer from depression. I know you had a panic attack yesterday and I know you had it because you care for me too. I know you're scared to death right now and I understand why you push people away. Those reasons may make sense to you, Nat, but they're wrong. *You're* wrong. I *do* know you. And I love you."

"Stop saying that!" she yelled. "Stop saying those stupid, useless words! Damn Teagan. Damn her for telling you all that."

"This isn't Teagan's fault. *You* should have told me, Nat. We're friends. We're—"

Her temper broke in two. Her nerves frazzled until the ends were snapping like a broken electrical wire. "We're *not* friends. We're nothing, Ewan. Nothing! Not now. Not ever. Your five minutes are up. Get away from that door."

"Natalie."

"Get. Away. From. The. Door."

She wasn't sure what he saw in her face. She could only imagine what sort of raving lunatic was reflected in his eyes. She felt caged in, trapped, and she was ready to claw her way out of this place with her own nails.

He unlocked the door and silently moved aside.

Her breath caught in her chest at his gesture. He was letting her go.

She stepped through the door and then, because her heart refused to leave without making one last stand, she turned. Saw the agony in his face. She made herself look at him and then said, "I'm sorry. I'm so sorry," and she walked away.

SEAN CARRIED her suitcase down to the waiting taxi the next morning. Keira had offered to drive her to the airport but she was anxious to make her break from this place, this family, as quickly as possible. As she descended the stairs, she was surprised to find most of the family gathered in the pub, waiting to say goodbye.

So much for an easy break.

Keira, Tris and Sean hugged her, said they looked

forward to seeing her back in Baltimore soon. She didn't have the heart to tell them hell would freeze over before she came back. Riley handed her a tiny bottle of tequila, telling her it was for the plane ride. She smiled and thanked her.

Teagan hovered in the background, guilt written on her face. Natalie couldn't find it in her heart to be angry with her friend. Teagan had merely done something Natalie didn't have the courage to do. She walked over and tugged on Teagan's long red hair. "I'll see you and Sky in Palm Springs next month, right?"

Teagan smiled. "And then back here at New Year's for the wedding."

Natalie felt a wave of panic at the thought of coming back. She seriously doubted she'd be able to make the trip. She hesitated, then nodded.

Pop stepped up, grinning and embracing her in a strong, fatherly hug that brought tears to her eyes. "We're going to miss you around her, Natalie."

"I'm still ahead on the fish count," she teased.

"I'll torment Moose with that information next time we're out."

"I'd be willing to call it even if he kisses the next fish he catches."

Pat laughed. "I'll be sure to snap a picture. Proof."

"I'll look forward to seeing it."

She stepped toward the door, turning to look back one last time. Looking for one face, wondering how she could dread and desire something at the same time. Ewan wasn't there. He wasn't coming. She'd hurt him irrevocably and she deserved his cold shoulder. She pushed away the pain that accompanied that thought. They all said one last goodbye and she waved before stepping out into the sunlight.

And he was there, resting against the cab, waiting for her.

"Ewan," she said, struggling to hide the tears rushing to her eyes. She put on her sunglasses to shield them from him.

"I wanted to give this back before you left." He reached out and she saw her camera in his hand. She'd forgotten about it.

"Thanks," she said, taking it from him.

"Goodbye, Nat." He stepped forward, placing a light kiss on her forehead. She held herself rigid as she forced her body not to melt into his. It would be so easy.

She smiled tightly. She didn't believe in saying goodbye. The word hurt too much, so she stepped around him and climbed into the cab. She wanted to look forward but she couldn't manage. She looked at Ewan as the taxi pulled away from the curb and she continued to stare at him until the car turned and he disappeared for good.

She pressed her head against the headrest and closed her eyes, letting the tears fall. For several moments she cried quietly as the buildings, the city flew by, each mile taking her farther away from Ewan.

They were halfway to the airport when she realized she was still clutching her camera in her hand. She toyed with the small thing briefly then turned it on.

She clicked through the pictures, pulling the small view screen closer, amazed at what she was seeing.

She didn't realize Ewan had been taking pictures of her the entire week.

There were a couple of her and Riley doing their hair and makeup in the bathroom last Saturday. Both of them laughing as Riley teased her blonde hair. Natalie grinned at the memory before clicking to the next shot. This one was taken by Aaron as she, Riley and Ewan all had shot glasses lifted to their lips. She laughed at the horrible wince on her face as the taste of the bitter liquor hit her tongue. She reached into her pocket and pulled out the tiny bottle of tequila Riley had given her. She smiled as she remembered the night, the dancing, the fun.

Clicking again, she discovered a photo of her with Pat and Moose, holding her first fish up as both men flanked her, looking as proud as if they'd caught it themselves. She laughed out loud and the cab driver glanced back at her as she flipped to the next photo and found Ewan had captured the exact moment she'd kissed the fish, Moose and Pat grinning like a couple of giddy fools over their prank.

There was another of her in her waitressing outfit, taking Mrs. Duvall's order. It was a simple picture, and she wondered how he'd taken it without her noticing.

There was one of her asleep in the hotel bed the first night they'd had sex, bright red rose petals covering the pillow beside her. He'd captured just her face and she was surprised to find true peace there. She didn't know she ever looked like that.

There was a shot of her singing karaoke, holding the microphone to her mouth, flirting with the cowboy in the purple shirt. She looked like someone else in that moment. Someone happy, someone special. Someone alive.

And then it hit her. She was the subject in every picture.

She was the focus, the center.

Ewan had done what he'd promised. He'd taught her how to live, given her a life—and he'd filled it with memories.

As they pulled up to the airport, Natalie knew she'd just made the biggest mistake of her life. Ewan was right. She'd let fear dictate her, rule her. She'd closed down after Yvonne's death, refusing to let anyone in for fear of pain.

She sat in the cab for several moments. The driver had gotten out, had pulled her suitcase from the trunk and now waited patiently on the curb. She looked out at the hustle and bustle of the airport and knew if she got on that plane, she'd never make it to Palm Springs without dying a million deaths along the way.

She couldn't leave. Couldn't live without Ewan. She didn't even want to try.

She rolled down the window. "Can you take me back?"

"Back?" the driver asked.

"To the pub where you picked me up. I want to go home."

The man looked at her like she'd lost her mind and she giggled. *Won't be the first time*, she thought, and she marveled that she could suddenly laugh about it. As the driver put her suitcase back in the trunk and pulled out, she closed her eyes and whispered to the only angel she knew.

"Help me, Yvonne. Help me. I love him. Please don't let me be too late."

LESS THAN AN HOUR had passed since she'd left but Ewan felt like it had been twenty years. He sat at the bar surrounded by his family and marveled over the fact they knew just what he needed. They left him in peace, but they stayed close. It was nearly ten and he knew he should move, knew he should get ready for the day, but his body felt too heavy.

Tris, Sean and Pop were hanging out behind the bar, putting bets on tomorrow's football game. His sisters were sitting at one of the tables behind him, looking at some *Bride* magazines. None of them were talking to him, but he knew if he gave even the slightest inclination of needing them, they'd surround him in a heartbeat, hold him up until he found his feet again.

Tris came over, stood across the bar from him. "You all right, bro?"

"Yep. Just got kicked in the teeth. It'll pass. In a couple hundred years."

"For what it's worth, I think she'll come back."

Ewan smiled mirthlessly and shook his head. "She's not coming back."

Tris bent toward him and held out his hand. "I'll bet you twenty dollars."

"Hate to take your money," Ewan said, returning his brother's clasp, appreciating Tristan's attempts at cheering him up. In this family, wagers were as sacred as holidays and he couldn't begin to list all the stupid things he'd bet over with his siblings in the past.

A feminine hand slapped a twenty dollar bill on the bar beside him and he turned, surprised, wondering how she'd come in without him noticing.

"Your brother's a cheating bastard." Natalie smiled at him. Though her tone was confident, wholly Nat, her face betrayed her nervousness. "Riley let me in on the restaurant side."

"Miss your plane?" he asked, trying to still the voice in his head, screaming that she'd returned.

She shook her head. "Never got out of the cab."

He grinned. "Damn."

She narrowed her eyes. "You're gloating."

"Yeah, I am. Just a head's up. I'm probably gonna be doing that for a while."

She laughed, her eyes drifting down. He could sense she was bracing herself for something.

"I love you." She blurted out the words and he was reminded of his own declaration the night before.

The devil in him prodded. She'd put him through hell the last two days. "What?"

She sighed, her eyes meeting his, proving she knew he was going to make her work for it. "I love you. I'm in love with you. Even though you are an annoying, perverted, cocky—"

He reached over as she spoke, halting her words with a kiss. As they broke apart, he rested his forehead against hers, loving the sweet smell of toothpaste still on her breath. "I love you too, Nat."

"I'm not easy to be with, Ewan. I get in these moods sometimes. My world goes sort of dark and it's hard for me to find my way back to the light."

He knew it was also hard for her to admit her faults. "Then I guess it'll just be my job to cheer you up."

"I'm not exaggerating."

He knew she was trying to stress how very real her problems were. She'd fought him too hard this week to walk into this without giving him a fair warning. Hell, she'd fought against this for three years and it was evident she wasn't going to let him proceed unless his eyes were wide open.

"I know you aren't, Nat. We'll work through it. Together. I promise."

"Yeah, well, I also live on the west coast."

"That one's gonna be tough." He looked around, realized his family was pretending not to listen, though he knew they were hanging on every word.

"No," she said. "It won't be. I've been thinking about opening up a second studio. Sort of becoming a chain."

His heart felt like it tripled in size at her words. "Baltimore could use a good photography studio."

"Yeah, I was thinking that too."

"You'd move here to be with me, Nat?"

"I'm tired of being alone. Tired of keeping people away. That may have worked in the beginning, after

Yvonne died. I think isolating myself helped me survive. Helped me move on. But now," she took a deep breath, "now it just hurts. I…I'd like to give this thing between us a chance. A real chance. We can't do that on opposite coasts."

He pulled her into his embrace, wondered how he'd lived his whole life never realizing this kind of intense love existed. He ran his fingers through her hair, tugged it gently until she looked at him. "I love you," he said.

She grinned. "I was wondering…" She leaned closer, whispering the next part, letting him know she was aware of their audience too. "Do you think Keira would take the lunch shift? I was hoping we could maybe…" She let him fill in the blanks as she gave him a wickedly sexy glance.

He pulled her closer, holding her head to his chest. "Hey, Keira. Think you can man the store today— both shifts? Nat can't keep her hands off me. It's gonna take me a little while to— Oof!" Natalie punched him in the stomach. "Hey, babydoll, that hurt."

"Oh, I'm gonna show you hurt in a minute."

Pop cut off their argument with a laugh. "You two get out of here. We can manage this place just fine. And Natalie…"

She turned to look at his pop.

"That's a hell of a catch you made there."

She laughed. "Think I should kiss him? Mark him as mine?"

Pop grinned. "I think you should definitely do that. Welcome home."

She smiled, tears gathering in her eyes as she reached out to hug Pop. "Thank you," she whispered.

"Now," Pop said, "go on. Do something special, something fun. It's times like these when life's meant to be celebrated."

EPILOGUE

Natalie stood beside Sky, listening as he and Teagan said their wedding vows. They were getting married in the pub, since that was where they met. Besides the family, there was only a small crowd of fifty close friends. They'd closed the pub shortly before Christmas so they could prepare for the ceremony. It was only a few hours before midnight—a new year.

Natalie felt Ewan's hand against her back and she smiled, glancing over her shoulder at him. It had taken her nearly two months of constant cross-country travel to get her ducks in a row, but by the beginning of December she'd managed to make her move to the east coast official and permanent. She and Ewan had decided to move in together. She'd suggested they were moving too fast, but Ewan pointed out he'd been patiently wooing her for three years, which, to his estimation, was too slow.

The past few weeks had been an exciting time,

unpacking, watching their home begin to take shape as her things meshed with his. She still got a thrill out of seeing her laundry mixed up with his in the basket, their toothbrushes hanging side by side. She'd become as obnoxiously romantic as the couple standing in front of her—and she was loving every minute of it.

Natalie watched as her business partner, Christine, snapped pictures of the ceremony. Natalie figured the paparazzi would work their asses off to try to steal a few, but she knew these photos would never be shared with anyone but trusted family and friends. The press would probably get a kick out of discovering Sky had chosen a woman to stand up as his "best man."

Ewan, Sean, Tris and Killian all stood behind her as groomsmen, while Keira as matron of honor held the flower girl, Catie, in her arms. Riley, as maid of honor, stood next to Tris and Killian's ladies, Lane and Lily. The ceremony was truly a family affair as Pop sat in the front row, beaming, his smile stretching from ear to ear. Beside him they'd left an empty chair, save for the white rose lying there—Sunday's seat.

Applause filled the pub as the minister pronounced them man and wife. Ewan snuck an arm around her waist, pulling her close. "Do you think it would be scandalous for a groomsman to kiss the best man?"

She turned in his arms. "Terribly scandalous," she said as she offered her lips. They kissed until Sean elbowed Ewan. "Knock if off, you two. It's not your turn."

Natalie laughed and turned back to hug Sky then Teagan. Soon the music started and the champagne began flowing. Just before midnight she sat down, removing her shoes to rub her aching feet. She'd danced with every male member of the Collins family, including Aaron, Sean's best friend Chad, and Killian and Lily's third, Justin. She was exhausted, exhilarated and happy.

She glanced across the room where Ewan and Tris were talking to Aaron. Riley had clearly over-imbibed. She watched Aaron lead Riley toward the stairs to the apartment.

Ewan joined her. "Tired?" he asked.

She nodded. "Riley okay?"

"She always takes things right to the edge. Tonight I think she went overboard. Aaron's gonna take her upstairs, get her to bed. If I know him, he'll stick around in case she gets sick. She put down way too much champagne. I worry about her sometimes."

Natalie remembered Teagan making the same comment. "She's lucky to have Aaron. He's a good friend."

"Amen to that. I don't know where she'd be without his steadying influence in her life. As bad as she is now, I can't begin to fathom what she'd be like without Aaron."

Natalie moved closer, surprised when Ewan pulled her off her chair and into his lap. "Ewan."

"It's almost midnight. I want to make sure I've staked my claim. You're going to be kissing me when that ball drops."

"You know? I don't think I've ever kissed anyone at midnight."

He grinned. "I like being your first…and your last."

The crowd started the countdown and Natalie felt a rush of excitement.

"Ten, nine, eight…!"

"I love you, hotshot," she whispered as the count continued.

"Five, four, three…!"

"I love you too, babydoll."

"Two, one! Happy New Year!"

Ewan pulled her face to his and she kissed him. She saw the flash of a camera out of the corner of her eye.

Another picture, she thought with glee. Another memory. Life was very, very good.

THANKS SO MUCH FOR READING! Be sure to check out the entire Wild Irish series.

Come Monday

Ruby Tuesday

Waiting for Wednesday

Sweet Thursday

Friday I'm in Love

Saturday Night Special

Any Given Sunday

Wild Irish Christmas

AND DON'T MISS the next generation, Wilder Irish.

Wild Passion

Wild Desire

Wild Devotion

Wild at Heart
Wild Temptation
Wild Kisses
Wild Fire
Wild Spirit
Wild Side
Wild Night
Wild Embrace
Wild Dreams
Wild Chance

FANS OF WILD Irish AND Facebook! There's a group for you. Come join the Wild Irish Facebook group for sneak peaks, cover reveals, contests and more! Join now.

BE sure to join my newsletter for a FREE Wilder Irish short story, One Wild Night.

## SATURDAY NIGHT SPECIAL

What do you get when you cross a gold-digging stripper, a down-on-her-luck hooker, an estranged husband, his knocked-up wife, a Wayne Newton look-alike taxi driver and one beleaguered Baltimore cop? A typical night in the life of Riley Collins—Vegas style.

Once again, it's Aaron Young to the rescue. Aaron's been watching Riley's ass forever—and he's wanted to spank it for even longer. Now, he's finally gets his wish —after he drags a drunken Riley to a chapel and makes it legit, of course.

*Excerpt:*

He sighed heavily. One question was tormenting him. "What are you doing in Vegas, Riley?"

"Gambling."

"Very funny." He grimaced, not amused by her joke.

"I'm having fun, Aaron. You know, that thing you've never quite mastered?"

He sucked in a deep breath and counted to ten. Riley constantly teased him about being a stick in the mud. He knew it was said in good fun, but this time her words felt more like an insult than a joke. Sometimes it sucked being regarded as the boring, responsible one among their group of friends.

Need a ride home from the bar? Call Aaron. Got a flat tire? Aaron will have a jack...and a spare. Moving? Aaron will lug all your shit down three flights of stairs and supply the truck to haul it.

A growl rose up in his chest. He was pissed off at Riley for thinking him so dull he wouldn't do anything as spontaneous as taking a weekend trip to Vegas.

"You seriously call hopping on a plane and flying to Vegas with Trevor Blankenship 'fun'? I call it fucking dangerous."

"Bullshit. I haven't done anything even remotely dangerous...yet. I called Keira and told her where I was and I didn't come alone. I came with a friend." Riley threw another dollar in the machine.

"You didn't call Keira until after you were already here."

"And like the good sister she is, she called you to come save the day. Right?"

"She was worried about you, Riley."

"I'm a big girl, sugar. A fact my family and you seem content to ignore."

"I'm not forgetting you're an adult. I'm just not overlooking the fact you're completely drunk in a strange town with Trevor and a hooker as your chaperones.”

Riley's gaze traveled from the slot machine to Aaron. “I told Trev she was a hooker, but he wouldn't believe me.” She took a long drink before setting the cup down and hitting the Spin button again.

“What are you drinking?” He picked up her glass and drained it. Alcohol suddenly seemed like a very good idea. He waved over the waitress and grabbed his own drink.

“Tasted like something with rum to me,” she said. “You better take it easy on that. I'm already wasted. If you keep pounding those down, who'll get us home?”

He shrugged and took another swig. Now that he was here, he wasn't in any big hurry to leave. “It takes a lot to get me drunk.”

“Yeah, well, maybe you should consider taking up the hobby. Drunk seems to be the best way to live in dreary Baltimore nowadays.” Her tone was sullen, belligerent, and he wondered at her words.

“Since when is Baltimore dreary? You love the city.”

She sobered up a bit and he was struck by the hint of sadness in her eyes. When he thought back on it, he realized the same look had been there often the past few months. Why hadn't he noticed it sooner?

“So I guess now I don't love the city. Dammit, I just can't do it anymore, Aaron.”

“Do what?”

“My life. I can't wake up in the same bedroom I've lived in since birth one more morning. I can't cook meals in that damn pub day in and day out anymore and I'm sick to death of partying with the same losers every Saturday night."

Her voice was filled with resentment, frustration, and he listened as the last detail—and he suspected the most important one—fell from her lips.

"I'm the last Collins kid at home. I'm it. The spinster sister," she added.

He burst into laughter. He knew she was being serious, but her words were so insanely funny he couldn't hold back his instinctive response.

Her eyes narrowed angrily. "What's so funny?"

"You," he said with a chuckle, "calling yourself a spinster. Two things I never thought I'd hear together in the same sentence. Riley Collins, the spinster." Repeating the words caused him to laugh again and some of the irritation he'd been harboring since leaving BWI that morning dissipated. Actually, simply finding her safe and sound had dispelled most of it.

"It's not funny. I've watched both my sisters find true love. They're living their happily ever afters while I'm still stuck at home alone with Pop."

"Happily ever afters? True love?" Aaron repeated. "Sounds pretty romantic for you, Riley. How much have you had to drink?"

"Ha ha. I've had too much and I'm gonna have more, but it doesn't matter. I'll still be fed up and lonely tomorrow."

Aaron looked at her dark brown eyes and felt a hope he'd never experienced stir inside him. "You said you never wanted to get married. You said it would cut in to your fun time, your independence. You've sworn off the entire institution since we were three."

"Yeah," she said. "Well, I changed my mind."

Aaron considered her words for a moment, and then gave in to the grin building in his chest. "Good."

"Good?"

He nodded, grasping her by the waist to set her on her feet. "Very good. Come on."

Saturday Night Special is available now.

# ABOUT THE AUTHOR

Virginia native Mari Carr is a New York Times and USA TODAY bestseller of contemporary romance novels. With over two million copies of her books sold, Mari was the winner of the Romance Writers of America's Passionate Plume award for her novella, Erotic Research. She has over a hundred published works, including her popular Wild Irish and Compass books, along with the Trinity Masters series she writes with Lila Dubois.

Follow Mari:
www.maricarr.com
mari@maricarr.com

www.ingramcontent.com/pod-product-compliance
Lightning Source LLC
Chambersburg PA
CBHW031245210726
48287CB00003B/901